Sideshows

stories by

B. K. Smith

LIVINGSTON UNIVERSITY PRESS

"Into the Sheminaun" appeared first in *The Sucarnochee Review*

Library of Congress Catalog number:
94-75777

ISBN 0-942979-15-X (cloth)
ISBN 0-942979-16-8 (paper)

Livingston University Press
Station 22
Livingston University
Livingston, AL 35470

cover art: Daniel P. Moore
book layout and design: Joe Taylor
Thanks to the following people for proofreading:
Tina Naremore, Ken Turner, Tammy Townsend, Claudia
Murphy, Jackie Dodgen, Melissa Holycross, and Carol
Waddell.

*The author wishes to express gratitude to Don Hendrie, Jr.,
Allen Wier, Tom Rabbit, Alice Parker, and all the guys from the
fiction workshop at the University of Alabama for their time and
attention to a large portion of this manuscript.*

*Thanks also to the following people for their support and
promotion of this work: Dr. Claudia Murphy, Tammy Townsend,
William Cobb, John Jolly, and Marthanne Brown.*

*Special thanks to Livingston University and Dr. Joe Taylor,
who said yes.*

Manufactured in the United States of America

Printed by Birmingham Publishing

CONTENTS

This collection is dedicated to the memory of my mother, Helen Castleberry Smith, who dubbed me B.K. the Poet when I was eleven. Through the years she encouraged my writing, and she believed in me.

SIDESHOWS

THE BARKER

It seems as though everything revolves around this wheel, at least for Jimmy. I found him here at 4 a.m. when I came back to the fairground from the city. After looking for him in several bars and diners, I found him here, circling all by himself on his double wheel—it, falling and pulling up again—him, staring straight ahead, pretending not to notice me. I *should've known*. This is where he always comes to get a new perspective on things. That's what he's doing up there now, since I pulled the bar and stopped him on top. He's figuring out a new angle, leaving me here ground level to sit and wonder if tonight was *all* my fault. I know he's mad at me because tonight I took something away from him. I'm the one who talked him into going into Kansas City, away from fairtown. It was his first trip out. I've seen a lot of the cities we've worked, but never Jimmy. He's always felt safe in fairtown, always cocky, confident and on top of things. I don't know exactly what happened in that room tonight, but I can guess, and my guess is that bitch hurt Jimmy pretty good—the way she was screaming at him. Now he's back here, trying to put his pride together. And he'll do it. He's never let anything get him down. He's always been in control, ever since I've known him.

My name is Jeff Ward, and some people would call me a "carnie," a trickster, or a shyster. I call myself a shrewd business-man. They'd call Jimmy a freak, but he likes to refer to himself as a showman. I remember the first time I met Jimmy thirteen years ago. He was eight, the same age as me, when Uncle Demps and I joined the fair. Even then Jimmy was in control. He knew he scared my shoes off the first time I saw him, with that giant growth on the left side of his face. It ran way out from under his black hair and down to his neck, like a second head, only bald. I thought it was just put-on until I finally touched it. It looked like a balloon, and I knew it would pop if I mashed too hard. But it was real skin, pink and firm. I remember Jimmy staring right into my eyes to see how I'd react. I was brave about it, but I still remember a sick feeling, and my knees getting weak, just before Jimmy grinned and told me it was bubble gum. He could blow his own bubbles anytime, he'd said.

Jimmy liked Demps and me right away, and it didn't take me long to warm up to him. He was always happy, smiling that wide smile that seemed to cover both of his faces. We were together all the time, playing circus, and pretending we were clowns or

B.K Smith

sideshow barkers. We liked to ride the Ferris wheel so we could get up high over the different cities—Houston, Atlanta, Louisville, and plenty of others. We'd drop peanuts on couples under us, who couldn't sneak a kiss for all the shells and nuts raining down on them. Jimmy loved the double wheel, and we both liked to get stopped on top. This was when we had our serious conversations about becoming fairowners, or ringmasters for P.T. Barnum's show. Every chance we got, we headed for the wheel. We liked to jump for our seats just as it started moving even though Roy, the operator, yelled at us for it.

Jimmy and I just grew up together, and while we were kids, I never paid much attention to his two heads unless he made me mad about something. Then I'd call him pig face or balloon head. But that didn't bother him. He'd just snort around, oinking like a pig, or tell me stories about how once he'd stuck a pin in his head to make it pop. Or he'd pace back and forth, telling me stories about how he'd taken a razor once and tried to slice off his other face, but that God had come down to him and told him not to do it—that it was a gift and there was magic in it. He'd have me half laughing, or half hypnotized, by his tales and gestures, and his faces would just seem to blend into one.

Jimmy was in our trailer every night, curled up next to me on the couch, listening to Uncle Demps' stories about the circus—about tightrope walkers and lion tamers. Jimmy would pretend he had a whip, and he would call me names like Rajah, or Samson, and order me to jump through a hula hoop that he called his ring of fire. Eventually, he moved in with us at the fairowner's request. Mr. Yudahl said Jimmy was becoming a burden to Fat Tina, who'd looked after him since he was a baby, and that he was getting older and needed men around him. He said Jimmy would be working in a few years, and Uncle Demps could train him in showmanship since Demps had been a first-rate ringmaster when he was younger and was now the barker for the sideshows.

Jimmy was already a first-rate ham. During the days, he'd make me sit on a stool while he paraded around, barking to his imaginary crowds, "See the wild boy, captured in the jungles of Africa. He smells like an animal; he eats like an animal—snakes, lizards, rats." I would beg Jimmy to let me be the barker, but he wouldn't, and he made me some new and different sideshow freak every day.

Sometimes Jimmy let me be in the spotlight, on nights when Uncle Demps told us over and over again about my mother.

Jimmy's eyes would get as big as my own when Uncle Demps talked. She was the most beautiful woman in the world, Demps would say, and she flew through the air like a graceful dove. She had fallen from the trapeze when I was two, so I never knew her except through Demps' descriptions of her black hair, as dark and sleek as a panther's coat, and her smile that made the whole big top light up before she glided across the air like an angel. I only knew the stories of her smooth and agile moves on the trapeze, her nights as a star, and her days as a warm, loving mother to me. Jimmy had never known anything about his own mother, so I let him share mine. He seemed to love her as much as I did. Neither of us had known our fathers. Mine, as Demps would say, was a good cat man, a good man, but he loved the bottle too much and ran away up North somewhere even before I was born. And Jimmy's, well, nobody ever talked about who his parents were. So we just latched onto the one pretty picture Demps had painted in our minds—Angelina, Angel of the Air—our daring dove of the trapeze.

Demps never told us about my mother's fall, or at least the details of it, until Jimmy and I were thirteen. I remember the night he told us. Afterwards, I went to bed, wishing he hadn't spoiled it for us. That night I dreamed of her, flying high above the crowd, reaching out with her smooth white arms to grasp her partner's hands—the miss—only a fraction of an inch away from safety. I dreamed of her falling, with no net below to trap her angel wings securely. I screamed, begging God to let me catch her. Then I woke up and felt myself reaching out in the dark for her hands. It was just like in Demps' story—all the crowd was quiet, holding their breaths, as the lights in the big top were shut off at her death. I thought I felt them, her hands, but they were Jimmy's. He was sitting on my bed and holding my hands real tight.

"Hey, you having a nightmare?" he asked.

"Yeah."

"About Angelina?"

"Yeah," I said as I wiped tears away from my face and tried to stop shaking.

"Boy I'm lucky," he said.

"Why?"

"Because I never had a mother to cry about, or have nightmares about. See, I think I was brought here by the fairies in a tiny golden Ferris wheel."

"You're stupid," I said.

"No," he whispered, "no, maybe I grew from seed like a potted

3   *B.K Smith*

plant."

By then Jimmy had me laughing a little. "Yeah, you're a plant, you elephant ears."

"Hey, you want I should sleep here with you and keep the nightmares away?" Jimmy was sliding in under the covers.

"Looks like you're going to anyway."

"Okay, I will but I need the whole pillow."

"No way," I said as I hit him over the head with my pillow. We scuffled and giggled until Demps switched on the light and told us to can the noise and go to sleep.

The next day, while Jimmy was out, I bugged Demps to tell me who Jimmy's parents were and what had happened to them. He finally told me that he'd heard that Jimmy's mother had been one of the showgirls in Mr. Yudahl's tent—one of the underdressed, overly made-up women that I stared at every chance I got. I loved standing in front of the girlie tent, watching their wriggling bellies and filmy costumes of golds and greens, and wondering what their skin felt like. And they watched me back, smiling at me, and running their tongues around their thick, red mouths like I was a lollipop on the midway. And one of these had been Jimmy's mother, or one like them. Demps said she had left the fair after Jimmy was born, and according to rumor, she had been scared of and disgusted with her new-born son. I was glad Jimmy didn't know. Better the fairies brought him, or that he grew from seed out of a clean earth.

When Jimmy and I were fourteen, we started to work a little around fairtown, to earn our keep, as Demps said. The social workers had stopped bothering us years before because every time they came nosing around, Demps would dress up fit to kill in a three-piece suit and would hire some horn-rimmed tutor to make us look studious. I remember one woman in particular, a social worker, who couldn't take her eyes off Jimmy as he worked out some made-up formula on the blackboard—a formula not unlike that used by respected nuclear physicist Arden J. Darnauch in his latest theory concerning relative fuel consumption modules, he'd said. And she watched, amazed, as Jimmy continued his act, scratching line after line of numbers and letters that did look like a pretty convincing formula. He knew she was watching, and he was loving every minute of it. After he finished, he put down the chalk, heaved a satisfied sigh, turned and walked over to her, bent down close to her face and said, "Truly, two heads are better than one. I have two brains." Even our tutor snickered a little as the woman, disgusted, nervously gathered her purse and briefcase and made her exit. We weren't worth it.

Social workers never really bothered us much because we had our own little world, and we moved it around too fast for them. Demps really did hire a few tutors for us, but Jimmy usually aggravated them with his know-it-all attitude until they quit. Sometimes I thought he did have two brains with all he knew. I guess he learned because he was always reading—to make himself a well-rounded person and a total showman, he'd say. Jimmy read a lot of trivia books, joke books, but his favorite were books on science. I only read what Demps made me read.

Jimmy and I liked growing up in fairtown, being on the fairground every night—all the people moving around, the flashing white lights, the smells of hotdogs turning and steaming inside the booths, and warm cotton candy on a stick. We liked the whine of the big motors and the screams of people who whizzed by upside down, strapped to seats in the air. We liked watching Demps at the sideshows, the way his gray hair glistened like angel hair under Christmas tree lights. We watched him move, one hand under his red suspenders, or tipping his hat to the crowd, and the other constantly pointing to the exaggerated paintings of freaks on the sideshow tent. He'd have the people shoving to hear his next words. "See the *Snakelady*, half *woman*, half *snake*. She slithers on her belly and tries to get at the crowd. Stay behind the ropes so she doesn't *strike* at you. See Samson the sword swallower slide the *fourteen-inch* blade down his throat. If he's careless he could *yank* out his heart. Come on in if you *dare*." The people couldn't wait to get into the tent to see Fat Tina, Big John—smallest man in the world—and all the others that Demps barked to the crowds. Jimmy and I couldn't wait to work full time and be a part of it all. Jimmy wanted top billing in the sideshow—"Jimmy the Two-Headed Boy—sees all—knows all—he can read your minds." I wanted to be like Demps, smooth and confident, at my own stand where I'd push three balls for a dollar, easy as pie, easy as one-two-three, just tip the lion's head over, win yourself a prize.

By the time we were sixteen, Jimmy and I were full-timers. I worked on body language, reading the crowds, knowing just when to pull some gullible guy in to win a big stuffed dog or bear for the girl who hung on his arm and looked at him as if she thought he could win her the world. I never thought of them as suckers. Jimmy had warned me about that. Just think of them as clients—people caught up in competition and gambles. He'd say, "You've got something they love; give it to them." I kept myself in tight jeans and clean white T-shirts that showed every muscle in my chest and arms—to look strong and in control—as Jimmy would say. I moved around like a cat, quick, and sure of myself. Only once was I caught off guard. I noticed a girl, about my age, staring at my fingers as they drummed the counter. I looked at my hands and was embarrassed by the dirty, ragged fingernails she frowned at. From then on I scrubbed and filed them every night.

Jimmy would come into the trailer all excited at the end of the night, about how he'd kept the crowd laughing at his two-heads-are-better jokes. Or, how he'd dazzled them with his mind reading. Of course he knew what they were thinking, he'd say; some of them are just too easy to read. He would sit there, rubbing that hard bubble of skin on the side of his head as if it were a treasure. "I've got power in this hump," he'd say. "Do you believe it? I can control the crowd with it. I can make 'em laugh, or I can make 'em stand there with their mouths open while I caress this jewel like it's a crystal ball and tell 'em about their lives."

I caught Jimmy's act every chance I got. He was a real showman, strutting back and forth across the stage like pure energy on two legs. I watched the faces that watched him, and they were trancelike. He would point out a person and tell him what he was thinking about the strange, intelligent, out-of-this-world creature who stood on the stage and spouted everything from jokes to philosophy. Or, Jimmy would tell another man what he was thinking about the woman beside him, and what he'd like to do with her later. The crowd loved that one. Jimmy would convince his audience that he wasn't really a freak. He was just ahead of our time. He was the look of the future, he'd say. Future generations would look like him when the brain began to expand and evolve further. He was more intelligent, he'd say, and more perceptive.

Demps said he'd seen other guys like Jimmy before, those who just sat on a chair, like a lump of shapeless clay on stage, and who only made the audience feel sorry for them. But not Jimmy. When he wasn't dazzling his show audience, he'd keep fairtown residents entertained during days off with his jokes and trivia. Sometimes I was a little jealous of his fame, but most of the time he pulled me in with all the rest, and I forgot about the envy.

There was only one bad incident during Jimmy's budding career. It was in Tupelo, Mississippi, on a muggy September night when the tents were like ovens and none of the small fans could cool the crowds. A young hefty guy in a football letter jacket almost threw a rock at Jimmy—a tough guy, wanting to show off for his girlfriend. I was there on my night off, so I was able to spot him before he did it. I tried to stop him, and I asked him to leave the show. We almost had trouble inside, but Demps came in and ordered the boy away from there. He tossed the rock at me instead. I wanted to go for him, but Demps held me back. The crowd was uneasy and shuffling toward the exit when Demps started his spiel about Fat Tina—600 pounds of woman and quite a bundle of love for any good man. I thought Jimmy would be upset when he came back stage, but he laughed it off. "Sticks and stones can break my bones and rocks can sure as hell hurt me," he said. I asked him if he wanted to call it quits for the night and he answered, "Are you kidding? They can't keep me down. I'm a first-rate showman. Don't you know? I've got the power to move 'em, especially that bad apple."

Later, after Jimmy finished for the night, we headed for our usual spot for relaxing and thinking—the double wheel. Jimmy wasn't saying much as the seat bumped and tilted and we started up in the warm night air. After a few rounds, we were stopped on top. He threw back the hood of his jacket. Jimmy had always sewn big hoods on his coats so he wouldn't spoil his show for the people on the midway, he'd said. He wore it in any weather. And I knew he had to be hot in it that night. He stared out at the lights of Tupelo, and I noticed a small spasm in his good jaw. I knew he was grinding his teeth like he always did when he was thinking hard.

"You upset about that guy at the show?" I asked.

"Him? Nah. There are a few like him. A guy has a sore spot, maybe an ugly spot down inside him. He comes in the sideshow, sees it out there in front of him, and he wants to laugh it away or rub it out for good. He pretends he leaves it inside the tent, but it crawls all over him again and settles underneath the skin, deeper every time, and he takes it right back out with him. That's the way I've got it figured. I read minds, remember?"

"Sometimes I think they hate us because we're so different," I said.

"They're not any different from us. They're all a little freaky. They just hide it better. They don't make a clean breast of it on the outside like I do. And when they come to the sideshow, they look real close and see a little bit of themselves up there on stage. It scares 'em sometimes."

"I don't mean just you. All of us. Maybe because we live a lot different than them. They stare at me, too."

B.K Smith

"But they don't have as much fun do they?" Jimmy laughed. "I mean they can't hide Snakelady's potent skin lotion and have her bring scales and curses on their children, can they?"

"No," I yelled out over the fairground as the wheel jerked and whizzed down again.

"And they can't cut out crash diets from magazines and pin them to Fat Tina's pillow, can they?"

"No." We both got louder as the wheel circled twice on top and shifted to the bottom. "And nobody has beat my system and knocked over the lion's head for a sure win, when I didn't want 'em to."

Jimmy was never serious for long. He always pulled out in time before conversations got too deep. He was in this world, he'd say, to entertain, and nobody likes a sour puss, or pusses. Even the night we talked about his mother, he didn't let it go too far.

We had ducked into the film tent that showed live births, and Jimmy had stood there in back of the hot, musty tent with his eyes frozen on the small screen. When I saw those little red arms and fists, squirming out from between two legs, I felt sick and had to go outside for fresh air and the safe smells of sawdust and popcorn. Later, on the wheel, he asked, "What'd you think of the film in there?"

"I don't know, pretty gory I guess. It was like that kid was fighting like hell to get outside and get some air. Like me," I laughed.

"Or maybe back inside."

"What?"

"I wonder if my mother had a hard time with me. I'll bet it hurt," Jimmy said.

"You? No way. Besides, you were hatched anyway, from a golden egg, right?" Jimmy smiled a little as he turned his face toward me, the fair lights flickering across the swollen knot just inside his hood.

"I'd like to try it again. Come out all smooth and perfect, so I wouldn't hurt her," he said.

"Who?"

"My mother, stupid. She worked in Mr Yudahl's tent. And I hear she was real pretty."

"Who told you that?"

"You think I'm blind and deaf? I'm the super freak, remember? I know what's going on."

"Oh," I said, as I sat there like a klutz, staring down at the midway.

"Man, I'll bet that was wild. She probably took one look at me and ran as far as she could go to get away from this ugly mug—or mugs."

"I don't believe that."

"Sure she did." Jimmy's face broke out into a big grin. "But that's okay. I'm glad it happened, because she gave me my trademark. Where would I be without my magic mountain here?" He patted his over-sized cheek. Jimmy was stubborn. He was always determined to laugh. I had never even seen him cry, and only once was he ever close to it. That was the day we buried Big John. On the way to the grave side, Jimmy was explaining that sometimes midgets' lives are as brief as their bodies, that they have a hard time surviving in a giant world. I thought I saw tears starting up in his eyes, but he blinked them back. Later, though, his soft, controlled voice did crack a little when he read the eulogy. It was pretty nice. Jimmy said, "Death is the biggest freak of all. It's tricky. It seems all distorted on the outside, but on the other side I think there's peace. Maybe even a new start somewhere. Just take a look at Big John's mound of clay. Seems like it keeps swelling doesn't it, as if maybe he plans to come up again—bigger next time—taller. You can't keep a good showman down, right? He's okay wherever he is. You can bet on it." And Jimmy stayed in control. He always did, whether the situation was bad or good.

When I turned twenty-one, I started nagging Jimmy about going into the cities with me. We were working in Birmingham the night of my birthday, which was three months after his. I was getting bored with fairtown, and even Candy, a girl in Mr. Yudahl's show, who had kept me pretty satisfied until then. And I was bored with riding that damned Ferris wheel with Jimmy all the time. I asked him to go with me. He refused. I did go out after midnight, hit a few bars, and was pretty bored there, too, but I never let Jimmy know that. I told him it was great.

I bugged Jimmy for months to go with me, see the sights, pick up some girls, and he finally told me flatly, "You're full of shit."

"What'd you mean?"

"You think I'm going out there. It's not the midway, stupid."

"You can wear your hood," I said.

"Sure, like a monk or something."

"Don't you want to find a woman?"

"In time," he said.

I knew I was being unreasonable with Jimmy, and selfish, but

9

B.K Smith

I couldn't help myself. He was always the big man around fairtown, and I guess I was just trying to show him how well I could function *anywhere*. I'd never gotten much attention from the crowds, or from anybody except Candy, and a few of the other girls. I guess Jimmy read me, like he did everybody, so he continued to frown and say no.

Tonight, Jimmy did go with me. It took everything I had in my bag of tricks to persuade him. And I guess he just wanted to shut me up finally. I promised him we'd go to a dark, quiet little bar in Kansas City, have a few drinks, walk a few streets, and come back to fairtown. Just after midnight, we got dressed, left the main entrance, and hit the streets. I was singing, "Kansas City, Kansas City here we come. We're goin' to Kansas City." And Jimmy was loosening up a little himself once he breathed in the city's cool night air and saw that it wasn't much different from walking the midway. We took a cab to the run-down hotel I'd checked out a couple of nights ago. I knew there were girls there for hire. I'd checked that out, too, with the bartender downstairs. I had big plans for Jimmy. We walked into the hotel's bar and took a booth in a dark corner near the back. I got us two bourbons from the bar and rejoined Jimmy, who was making sure his hood covered his face. He sipped his drink, slowly, and shifted around in his seat.

"Don't look so nervous," I said.

"Who's nervous?"

"You want to pick up some girls?" I asked.

"What? Hey, man, you said drinks and home, okay?"

"Are you scared?"

"Hell no, I'm just not in the mood. I'm tired."

"Sure you are."

"Okay, know-it-all, you find 'em and I'll screw 'em."

I could tell that Jimmy was getting mad at me, but I couldn't help myself. I had to show him I could be in control. I left our booth and went for refills. On my way back, I stopped at a table on the other side of the room. The bartender had directed me to two women who sat toying with their drinks.

"Hi, ladies," I said, trying to sound cool and glancing around to make sure Jimmy was watching. He was glaring at me.

"Hello, sugar," the blonde woman drawled as she ran her tongue around her lips. She reminded me a lot of the girls in Yudahl's tent who used to lick me up with their eyes when I was on the midway.

My voice cracked a little. "Uh, do you do anything? I mean,

do you take anybody?"

"For the *right* price. Why, baby, are you a little freaky or something?" The redhead teased me.

"No, but my friend is."

"Cost you a little more if he's kinky, baby. That him? The Eskimo over there?" The blonde woman nodded her head in Jimmy's direction.

"Yeah. No, I mean he's really a freak."

"Head trips don't bother us. We drop some acid ourselves now and again. He'll just have to bring his own," the blonde said as she picked up her purse and started moving out of the booth. "You *boys* come on up in a few minutes—you 302, him 303. We'll be ready."

"Wait," I said, trying to explain.

"Not too long," the redhead said, "we might get impatient." Both women started up the stairs, and I walked back over to Jimmy with our drinks.

"What was that all about?" he asked.

"Well, it's all set. I gave them the scoop. They want us to come up. You go to room 303."

"You told them *everything*?"

"Honest injun. It's cool. Just have yourself a ball. It's on me. You ready?" I moved out of the booth.

"I'm going to finish my drink. Then I'll be up. Where will you be?"

"Room 302," I said, as I winked and headed for the stairs.

When I got to 302, the blonde was waiting for me. She was lying on the bed in a thin blue robe, parted slightly, revealing a strip of smooth white skin down her middle.

"A twenty should do the trick," she laughed.

"Oh, I almost forgot," I said, and I placed a twenty dollar bill on the dresser. As I began to undress slowly, she reached to the small lamp on the bedside table and switched off the light.

"Think that'll speed things up, baby. I'm a working girl, you know."

I slipped in between the cool sheets and felt her arms go around my neck. She pressed herself against me, and I wondered, for just a moment, how Jimmy was doing before I began to make love to her. She wasn't much different from Candy, just older, and I reacted the same as I always did. I liked the way her legs felt against my hips, the softness of her breasts, and the heat inside her body as I entered her. Same as always, it took me outside myself.

B.K Smith

I seemed to float somewhere in the room and watch the show like an awe-struck bystander on the midway. Then, as usual, I was pulled in as easy as pie, as easy as one-two-three, trying to tip the lion's head, over and over, until I won the prize. I don't know how long it was before I heard the shouting from next door.

"What the hell is this? You're a freak!" I heard the redhead scream in the next room. I heard glass crash against something and heard her yell again, "Is this some lousy joke? Get out. Get outta here you sicko. Sicko creep!"

I was scrambling into my pants when I heard Jimmy shouting from the hallway, "Big deal, bitch. You're not the first, and you're sure not the best." And then the door slammed shut. Jimmy was gone by the time I got my clothes on and was out of the room. The redhead's face was white, and tightened up like a drum skin. She started beating me with her fists as I ran toward the stairwell. I had to find Jimmy. How could I have been so stupid and mean to set him up like that.

I looked for Jimmy everywhere—in bars along the street, in alleys—but I knew where he'd gone. Fairtown. I just didn't want to face him. Around 3:30 I took a cab back to fairtown. I wandered around the grounds, kicking empty beer cups and punching my fists into the sideshow tent—rights to the Snakelady's stomach, lefts to the sword swallower's chin. I hated myself as I walked on down the midway. I had been a selfish, jealous son-of-a-bitch who didn't deserve Jimmy's spit. I was kicking myself pretty hard when I spotted him, all alone, riding the double wheel. That's when I walked over and looked up at Jimmy—coming down, moving up again.

"How're you gonna stop it?" I yelled to him.

"I'm not," was all he said before I put my hand on the cold steel of the control bar and stopped him on top—to let him think and grind his teeth. I knew he'd be okay. That's when I sat down to wait, and think a little myself.

It's been about an hour now and not a word from Jimmy. All I hear is an occasional squeak from one of the metal seats when the wind blows through the wheel. I could let him sit up there and sulk until dawn. Or, I could pull him down and join him. It might be nice to watch the sun come up over Kansas City, and over fairtown, before we pick it clean and head for Little Rock.

AND THE RAINS CAME DOWN

I remember the first time Leda announced plans to kill her mother. It was on a hot, late August morning while we were waiting for the first school bus of our eighth grade year at Kipling Jr. High. All the kids at the bus stop were sleepy-eyed and drowsy except Leda. Her eyes were wide and bright with excitement as she drummed her knuckles white on her books. She seemed impatient for something more than a late bus as she flipped her pigtails away from her face and shifted from one foot to another. I was curious about her mood, and as her best friend, I felt it was my duty to ask what was going on.

"I missed—that's what," she answered, "but I'll get her next time."

"Get who?" I asked.

"My mother. I had her. Oh boy did I. She was making me wash dishes again, and I reached down in the suds for the butcher knife, pulled it out with both hands, raised it over my head, and she moved. She put the salt up in the cabinet, closed the door and moved. Can you believe it? I missed her this much."

Leda measured the distance with her thumb and forefinger, and I stared at it in shock just before the bus pulled up and Leda pounded up the steps ahead of me. I followed her to the seat to find out more.

"Stop it, James Calvin. Keep your creepy hands off me. I'm in no mood for you today." Leda yelled and slapped at James Calvin Mills, who always sat behind her on the bus to pull her hair and flirt. He shrugged his shoulders, but slid back in his seat as if he knew she meant it.

"Why in the world did you try to kill your mother?" I whispered.

"Because she's really done it this time. Daddy left this weekend. For good."

"Where'd he go?"

"I don't know. Away from her, for sure. The nag. They had another fight. He didn't even tell me goodbye. He was slamming things around, and I was too scared to get out of bed. I heard him go out the front door, and I heard *her* yell good riddance. Then I got up."

"What happened?"

"She said he was gone. She said it was for the *best*. Can you believe that? Daddy left and she didn't even cry. She just stared at me funny, walked into the bedroom, and started picking up old shirts and socks he didn't pack."

"Nothing else happened?"

"Nope. She tried to hug me once, but I wouldn't let her touch me. She knows I hate her. She got what she wanted. She finally ran Daddy off. Judas Craps, what did she expect from me."

Leda spouted her favorite phrase, her answer to all bad situations, the words she'd been whipped with switches many times for saying. And she tore at her fingernails with her teeth, tearing them off in little slivers and biting them down into the soft quick of her skin. Her mother had always scolded her for that, too. I turned to stare out the window as the bus bumped along the road to school, trying to think of something smart to say. I was thinking about hating Mrs. Reed myself. Leda's mother was a really strict woman, who was always fussing at Leda for something, and who kept switches on top of her refrigerator in case Leda got out of line. I thought about how mean she could be.

I thought of Leda's daddy, too, and how he hadn't seemed like such a bad man when we were younger. He had taught our Sunday school class and had made going to church fun. He made us love the songs about Jesus—how he loved all the little children of the world—or songs about Daniel in the lion's den, or David and his slingshot that brought the mean giant Goliath to his knees. And then there was the song Leda and I especially liked. As we sang, "The rains came down, and the floods came up," we'd lower our arms from above our heads quickly as the rain fell down, then lift our palms slowly by levels as the floods came up. Leda's daddy would always provide a picture to go with every song. Again, our favorite was the one of old Noah, with the long gray beard, standing on the deck of his ark after the flood, with a dove on his forefinger. Leda's daddy would say that all the evil of the world was washed away and nothing but innocent animals and good people lived, two by two, perched high on a dry rock, safe and secure inside the boat. We learned later that her daddy hadn't always gotten the stories right, or put the right pictures with the right songs, but he had kept us happy. After awhile Leda's daddy started leaving church right after Sunday school, and then he stopped coming at all. My parents said he drank too much and didn't need to be in church, especially not teaching the children. They said Leda's mother deserved better, that she was such a fine Christian woman. I was too confused to know who was right, but Leda wasn't. That day on the bus she had decided that her mother was the guilty party, and I just sat quietly and listened on the way to school.

"You know what she tried to make me do Saturday morning?"

I shook my head.

"She tried to make me help her pack up Daddy's stuff in boxes and carry them to the garage."

"Did you?" I asked.

"No way. I told her she could do her dirty work herself."

"You got away with that?"

"You bet. I thought she was gonna lay into me with one of her tree branches, but she just took a deep breath and started lugging the boxes out one by one. She told *me* to start cleaning the house."

"Did you?"

"Yeah. I did that. Half way. She kept coming in to check my work, like after I cleaned the bathtub, she came in to inspect it. When she bent over, I picked up the plunger, pulled it back, and almost rammed her in the butt with it."

I laughed when Leda sucked in her cheeks like a plunger and slammed her fist into her lunch sack. "Boy that could really kill a person," I said. She didn't hear me.

"I wanted to suck her into it and squash her up and down in the toilet until she drowned, and flush her away. Judas Craps, Daddy was only gone for a few hours, and it was like she was trying to clean up everything he'd ever touched. Like he'd gotten everything all dirty."

I was glad to reach school that day, and I hoped Leda would soon forget her plans for murder during school, but she didn't. On the way home, and in the days that followed, she rattled off hundreds of methods—from her own father's shotgun (justice she'd call it), to poison, to leaving a bar of soap on the back steps so her mother would slip and fall when she carried out the wash to the clothes line. Once Leda had almost gotten her mother snakebitten. Leda was racing her turtles, Myrtle and Jeffrey, on the hot sidewalk in front of her house when she spotted what seemed to be a peculiar stick standing up out of the ground in the shrubbery on the right side of the walkway. She ran to her house, yelling to Mrs. Reed that there was a snake in the bushes on the left side of the front walk. Her mother had gotten a hoe and had managed to find the snake and kill it, much to Leda's dismay.

Leda even got me involved in her schemes one Sunday afternoon when she came over to my house. She brought dozens of pencils with her, and instructed me to help her pound the lead into a fine crystal powder with a small hammer. She'd heard about lead poisoning and intended to sneak it into her mother's food. I wondered then if Leda was really serious about killing her mother, or if pencil lead could really do the trick. I wasn't sure, but I helped her anyway, and I helped her pack it up later in a small brown paper bag. We lay on the bed afterwards, looking up at the ceiling, and I wondered what God thought of it all. I was sure he'd understand. I was mad at Mrs. Reed myself, especially after the way she had treated Leda on Halloween night.

Leda and I had gone trick or treating with James Calvin, Leonard Murphy, and Sue Ellen Lowry on Halloween. And after the usual tricks and treats, we were bored. We gathered up all the cans we could find and stacked them in the road below Kipling Ridge. We sat on the hill in the moonlight, watching our makeshift architecture catch slivers of moon as it glistened ominously, awaiting the first car. We rolled on our backs, laughing, as cars swerved to miss the cans, or plowed right through them, causing a shower of aluminum in the air. One man got out of his car and screamed curses to the night before he roared away.

"I think that was Mr. Lawson," Leda said as she lay on her back in the grass, staring up at the sky. I wasn't sure if I saw reflections of stars dancing in her eyes, or a mischievous twinkle she'd sparked herself. "He sounded a lot like Daddy," she said, "but Daddy never yelled at *me* like that. He was always taking me places and buying me stuff. He'd buy me dresses and call them pretty wings for his pretty angel. Sometimes at night he'd let me lay across his lap while he watched T.V., and he'd rub my back until I went to sleep. Nobody knew Daddy like I did. He wasn't always yelling and drinking like everybody says. He only hit Momma one time, and she deserved it. And he never once yelled at me for anything, or spanked me. He couldn't stand to he'd say."

"Do you think he'll come back?" I asked.

"No. He's gone. She saw to that."

The man on the road had been Leda's neighbor, Mr. Lawson, because later he brought Leda's mother storming up to the ridge where we were all huddled, awaiting the next explosion of cans. Mr. Lawson just shook his head as if there was nothing he could do for such bad children, but Mrs. Reed embarrassed Leda good in front of all her friends.

"Get in the car, young lady, if I can even call you that. This is the last time you'll ever go anywhere without me," she said.

"Judas Craps, Momma, we weren't doing anything," Leda

whined.

"Stop that. Don't you ever say that again, or I'll wash your mouth out. You sound just like *him*. Come on." Leda's mother grabbed her arm and headed her toward Mr. Lawson's car, and the rest of us stood back and watched.

"Go to hell," Leda screamed, as she yanked her arm away and fell into the weeds at her mother's feet. "You just go straight there."

Mrs. Reed jerked Leda up and slapped her hard. Then she drew her hand up to her chest as if she'd burned it on Leda's cheek. "Damn," she said quietly as she turned and got into Mr. Lawson's car. "Damn him," she said.

None of us could believe what we saw, or that Mrs. Reed had actually said those words. I guess Leda couldn't either because she got into Mr. Lawson's car when he told her to, and they drove off. The rest of us scattered and slipped away to our own homes— bewildered. So, later, when Leda came over to my house and asked me to help her grind up pencil lead, I didn't feel too bad about it. I figured her mother deserved it after slapping Leda around in front of her friends.

A couple of months after Leda's visit that Sunday afternoon, she told me on the school bus that her father had sent the final divorce papers.

"The divorce papers came this weekend," Leda said.

"I guess that means it's really over, huh?"

"Yep. The end. Zip. Close the book. Daddy's gone." Tears balanced just on the bottom ledge of Leda's eyes, but she blinked them back. She wouldn't weaken.

"What did your mother say?"

"Nothing. She just signed the papers on Saturday. I heard the witch moaning in her bed Saturday night."

"I guess she's sorry now, huh? Maybe she'll change her mind and ask your dad to come back home."

"Hell, no. That's not it. Her stomach just hurt. It's the stuff in the pepper shaker. Judas Craps, she's been eating lead for weeks."

I was a little afraid of Leda at that moment. Her face was so red with anger. I wanted to make a joke of it all like I always had, but all I could manage was a scared half laugh before she began her steady tirade again.

"God, I hate her to death. You better be glad you and your parents were out of town yesterday. You should've seen them in church. They all knew. This whole rotten, stinking town is on her side. They treated her like some kind of hero or something, clucking around her like old biddies, patting her shoulder, saying they were glad it was over."

I listened, and wondered what would happen if Leda's mother did die. I wondered what they would do to Leda.

All through high school, Leda continued her threats. I didn't let it bother me much anymore. By then I figured Leda was just letting off steam or playing out some imaginary vengeance in her mind. After all, she hadn't been successful, so I didn't think she really intended to succeed at murder. She would still come over to my house, sit on my bed, punch my teddy bear's face until his button nose slipped sideways, and storm about her schemes—how she had been putting ground glass in her mother's food or oil on the back steps so her mother would slip. When I teased Leda about her failures, she would just say all those were practice sessions, little tortures before the big finale. She was waiting for the perfect moment.

It was in the August after our senior year that she carried out her final plan. We were working on a fair project at Leda's house when she gave me the shock of my life. Our project was to raise shrimp under controlled conditions. She had ordered the eggs months earlier, and we were going to observe them with an old microscope from a biology kit she'd had since tenth grade. Leda and I were to keep the shrimp alive in the briny solution for as long as possible after they hatched. On the night they began to hatch, Leda called me to come over. I was sitting there, watching the tiny shrimp squirm out of their eggs, when Leda gave me the news.

"Aren't they cute with their little tails whipping around in the water?" she asked. "They look kind of like sperm, don't they? And little embryos before that, don't they?"

I mumbled a yes they do as I kept peering into the glass container full of baby shrimp. Leda placed some of the unhatched eggs on a slide and told me to observe them through her microscope.

"That's what it looked like at first," she said.

"What what looked like?" I asked, adjusting the microscope.

"My baby."

"Your what?" I looked up at her.

"My baby. I'm pregnant."

"Is this a joke?" I asked, a little nervous about the answer I might get.

"Nope. This is it. This is the big one. This will kill her for sure."

"Is it James Calvin's?" I asked her quietly. I couldn't believe my ears. It had to be another threat, just another imaginary attempt to destroy her mother. I knew she still hated Mrs. Reed as much as ever, but I didn't think she'd go that far.

"Nope. Guess." Leda danced around the room, glancing at me over her shoulder each time she turned her back, to see my reaction. She stopped, finally, and faced me. "Nah, you'll never guess. It's Bubba Swanson."

"Who?"

"Bubba Swanson. Big Daddy."

"You mean that guy from Preston who rides a motorcycle like he's some kind of hell's angel?"

"That's the guy. But he's no angel."

"You're nuts. When did all this happen?"

"Oh, I've been seeing him on the sly. I decided to do it after the prom. I swore that was the last time she'd ever make me go out with James Calvin, that creep. She thinks he's so perfect—such a good church-going boy. Wonder what she'd say if she knew James Calvin left his wallet lying around school for people to find it full of rubbers, or if she knew he tried to get in my pants after the prom."

"I just can't believe this. When? I mean where did it happen?"

"Judas Craps, you want all the gory details? It just happened— a few times—I sneaked out at night to meet him. You don't believe me?"

"I don't know."

"Well, just check with Dr. Jemison. He told me today—the old rabbit died. And pretty soon it'll be all over town. And pretty soon she'll know—then wham. That ought to do it."

"Do what?" I asked angrily. "This isn't going to kill her. It's just going to wreck your own life. Sure, it'll hurt her, and I don't understand that either. I never really have. I got over all that *crap* years ago. Your mother's not *that* bad."

"Not you, too. Just like all the rest of this egg-sucking town." Leda glared at me, but I went on.

"Grow up, Leda. I went along with you all these years. Hate my mother, kill my mother. I've listened to all your ravings, but now you've really done it. I wish I had said something sooner."

"I wish I'd known you sooner, *friend*. You want to know why I want her dead?"

19

B.K Smith

"Because she ran your precious father off, that's why. Well, maybe he wasn't so precious. I know he was a drunk. Everybody knows it. Maybe your mother couldn't stand it anymore."

"You just shut up." Leda drew her hand back to slap me. Her lower lip trembled, but she stilled it with her teeth. Then, slowly, emphasizing each word, she said, "I want her dead because she wanted me dead."

"What does that mean?" I asked.

"Because the night my father left I heard her yell that maybe she should've had *that abortion* years ago. She wished she had. The hypocrite. Maybe she *should've* killed me. Then she wouldn't have had to spoil her prissy, self-righteous body with this sin." Leda dug her thumb into her chest.

"Oh, God, Leda, I didn't know. I'm sorry." I tried to put my arms around her. I couldn't think of anything else. She pushed me away. "Leda, maybe it wasn't your mother's fault; she was just mad that night. Maybe your father was the one. Maybe he wanted her to have the—abortion."

"Stop it," Leda screamed as she slapped her hands against her ears. "Get out, Miss Goody Two Shoes, Miss Know-It-All. You're just like the rest of them. Go. Get out."

I knew Leda meant it. I slammed out of the front door of her house and almost ran into Mrs. Reed, who was coming back from a quilting session at the church. I think she spoke, but I wasn't sure at the time. I walked home in the August heat, feeling as if the town were pressing down on me like an iron. I listened to the steady, brittle buzz of insects in the trees, like power lines cut in half, and watched grasshoppers try to pump their dry, dusty legs in the weeds. And, as I walked, I thought maybe Leda was right. Maybe I was just like the rest of them, self-righteous and stuffy, condemning her father and running him out of town. I was mad at the whole town of Kipling, and I was mad at Leda's mother, and even her father too, for driving my best friend to such an awful decision. But, mostly, I was just mad at myself. I knew Leda was hurting, and I didn't know how to soothe that kind of pain. I tried to call her when I got home, but she refused to talk to me. She wouldn't answer any of my calls in the days that followed, and when my mother heard the news, I wasn't allowed to call at all anymore.

Leda was right. Everyone did find out. All of Kipling stirred with rumors that summer. Leda stopped coming to church, and Mrs. Reed sat alone with her head down, her face tired and drawn. James Calvin spread nasty rumors that Bubba Swanson was a "homo" and that it couldn't be his baby. Some of the meaner boys even hung a plastic doll by the neck in a tree in front of Leda's house. By the end of August, Leda was gone. Some said she rode off with a gang of Hell's Angels. Others said she took the train up north to have an abortion.

I eventually discovered where she had really gone when I got a letter from her at Christmas, forgiving me for my blunders, she said. She was in a home for unwed mothers in the East, where Bubba Swanson had left her months before. She didn't write much but said that she was healthy, happy, would keep her baby, and would love it like crazy. I called Mrs. Reed with the news, but she said she didn't want to see the letter. Later, I received another letter in May, with a picture of *two* baby boys enclosed. Leda was happy and working to support her "big" family, she wrote. I took the letter and photo to Mrs. Reed, hoping for some response, maybe a wish that her daughter would come home. She read the letter, but said nothing but a polite thank you. I did think I saw a faint smile when she stared at the picture, but she quickly handed it back to me and brushed her hands on her apron as though they might be dirty.

I heard from Leda several times over the years, and with each letter her tone seemed to be lighter, more loving. I wrote to her about my job in Fields Dress Shop and about how people had said I had a talent for clothes. I told her I had even considered leaving town several times to pursue a career in buying, or even designing, but that I'd gotten cold feet every time. She teased me once, on the phone, when I called to tell her that Leonard Murphy and I were engaged. Leda said I'd probably stay in Kipling forever, married to the preacher's nephew, and have a houseful of perfect little Murphys. And she was right. I knew then that I probably would.

When Leda wrote, there wasn't any hate in the voice I read, just notes about the boys and minor problems, and plenty of love for them in every word. She did say that it was hard sometimes, bringing up the twins all alone, trying to be a mother and father, making the right decisions. She had even taken them to church and had taught them all the silly songs we used to sing, she said, and could I believe it. There was never any mention of her mother, but I had a feeling that Leda wasn't sending pictures of the twins just for me. Each time I got a letter, I visited Mrs. Reed, and each time she tried to seem annoyed. But, eventually, she even kept a picture or two, because I wouldn't leave her alone until she did, she'd say. I felt a little sorry for Mrs. Reed. I could tell that she wanted to give in sometimes, but she was a stubborn, hard woman who still didn't know how to communicate with her daughter.

For seven years I kept hoping things would change between Leda and her mother. I'd hoped that I could bring them together, but then it was too late. Leda's mother was dead. She was killed in her garden right after a storm. August is usually a bone-dry month in Kipling, but this year was different. There were flashfloods and electrical storms, and the town was washed by rain. Mrs. Reed was struck by lightning while harvesting the remains of flooded vegetables from her garden on August 20. Her neighbor, Mr. Lawson, said he was watching her from his window when, suddenly, the bolt came streaking down on her like nothing but lightning. It had ripped her dress, torn off the sole of one shoe, and had left her bruised, twisted, and dead in a muddy row of squash. And Leda came home for the funeral.

I sat next to Leda and her two boys during the church services. They looked so much like her with their dark, smooth skin and periwinkle blue eyes, such a striking contrast to the rich rings of black hair that curled around their ears. She tried to keep them still and quiet during the services, bringing her forefinger to her lips when one shifted restlessly in his seat or the other clacked the heels of his shoes together. I could tell she loved them. She answered their whispered questions softly and with a smile that told them everything would be all right, that she would answer their puzzled looks in time. The boys squirmed in their seats, aware of all around them, wriggling with life and confusion. They were different somehow from the other children in church, who were used to sitting next to their mothers like toy soldiers or polished China dolls.

The boys reminded me of Leda and me when we were their age—restless and anxious to be freed from the hard, wooden benches—eager to throw off the quiet bonds of religion for a game of tag outside. But Leda and I were always there, too, held captive until the last song was sung and the last prayer prayed. We'd liked Sunday school okay, when her father was there to help us make things, or color in biblical storybooks, or sing children's songs. But the fun stopped after Sunday school, when Leda and I sat next to our mothers, listening to grown-up words about sin from Reverend Murphy up front. We thought we must have sinned when we tried to sleep against our mothers' arms and were pinched awake. And we were punished many times for our sins of talking during the sermon, or waving our collection plate money high above our heads for everyone to see what we were giving. Leda and I had considered church and all its restraints with the same puzzled looks that I saw on the faces of her twins.

I was proud to sit next to Leda and her boys in church, and I suppose I was a little defiant, too. I expected to see cool curious looks from friends of her mother. I was sure they would frown on Leda and consider her a thankless hussy, who'd left her mother alone and in shame to run off with the no-good boy who'd gotten her pregnant. I admired Leda for leaving Kipling when she did and even more so for having the strength to come back. I knew her better than the others, her real story, why she had to leave when she did, before the hate inside consumed the new life she was carrying.

But I seemed to be the only one watching Leda during the funeral services. Her face, framed by short, dark curls in place of the hair that once fell long across her shoulders, seemed softer than it had before. There were no hard lines of hate etched around her mouth and eyes as I had expected after all those years of malice toward her mother. Her fingers played with a thin, white handkerchief in her lap. It was completely dry, and I wondered if it would stay that way. I wondered if Leda would shed any tears for her mother. Was she happy that she'd finally gotten her wish after so many years? I expected Leda's return to turn Kipling upside down, but I was surprised. There was no hostility. It seemed they had all forgotten. The townspeople were exceptionally nice as Leda walked with her two boys to the graveside. Everyone offered condolences, and James Calvin, carrying his own two-year-old daughter, tousled the hair on one of the twins and said Leda had two fine-looking boys. I couldn't believe it.

I sat next to Leda and her sons under the tent and listened to Reverend Murphy's words merge with the gentle tapping of rain on the canvas. And then I heard it—a low but distinct "Judas Craps" coming from Leda as she stared into her lap. Reverend Murphy's wife, standing behind Leda, patted her shoulder and said, "Yes, honey, Jesus cares."

Leda and I looked at each other, then smiled. There was actually a tear easing its way down her cheek when she said, "I guess she wasn't so bad."

"No, nobody's *so* bad." I reached across one of the twins and took her hand. The boys stared, puzzled, first at me, then Leda, then at our hands, before they turned their attention back to the slow drip from the tent roof and the small stream of water on the plastic flooring at their feet. I felt good about Leda, and the town, as though there was a new order in her life, and ours. As if maybe the tears and the rain had finally washed all the hate away. I listened to Reverend Murphy drone "from dust to dust" and watched the twins make circles in the water with the tips of their shoes.

LIZARD TRICKS

I.

Jake lay on the couch, stretched the full length of it and more, as he rubbed his feet together, one on top of the other. He brought his right foot up to his knee to observe a small hole in the heel of his sock. Mitzi would've scolded him for that. "No matter how many pairs of socks I buy you, you're going to wear one with holes in it." And she would've never let the white ones get dingy like this, but he just couldn't seem to get the hang of making things white and bright on wash day.

He lifted a book from his chest, *Revolutionary Road*, one he'd been trying to finish for months. He never got past Frank Wheeler's stone path, the scene where Frank raised the shovel and imagined it coming down on his kid's foot. And then there was the severed foot in Frank's mind, covered with red dirt and blood. "Damn it, Frank, it's not real! Don't yell at your kid, you idiot. It's not real! You're just too confused to know the truth."

Jake stared at the pages, read the same words over and over until they blurred. He couldn't go on, couldn't finish it, no more than Frank Wheeler could build his stone walkway, so he'd have something solid under his feet. Jake slammed the book shut, no need to mark the spot. The corner of the page had been folded down too many times. He threw it on the glass coffee table, one of the few pieces of furniture Mitzi had left with him after the divorce. It was one of the things, other than him, she didn't want.

Jake threw his arm over his eyes to shut out the late summer sun filtering through a crack in the drapes leading to his patio. And he began to daydream again, his favorite thing to do in the past months, a necessity in his life, as much so as food or breathing. He took out his obsession, laid it in his mind's hand, observed it, turned it over and around, fondled it, and pulled it close to his chest—held it out again to study it like a Rubik's Cube, complex and time-consuming, but worth the effort. It was his one sweet memory of Penelope, the seductress, enchantress, dark mysterious woman who'd stolen his heart away, the woman who'd taken his soul and left him with an empty shell, fragile and as easily shattered as glass. She had swept him off his feet and had left him with no foundation, no direction, no future—only vague promises, taunts, and this obsession, this memory of her hand on his face, her lips at the edge of his mouth, her sweet smile promising more and more.

B.K Smith

Jake let his obsession take him back, back to a year ago when he first met Penelope. It was the first time he'd ever been South, or to Oxford, Mississippi. During their 15 years of marriage, he and Mitzi had been to Europe, Hawaii, and out West, all over the North and Northeast, but never to the South. He had taught one semester in Iowa, but most of his life he'd taught literature, writing classes, and had shared his poetry in the North. He'd met Penelope's mother Vella in January at a writer's conference at Breadloaf in Vermont and had fallen in love with this witty, charming, rosy-cheeked woman of 60 with hair the color of clouds before a winter storm. He had invited her to dinner at his home in Old Greenwich and later to see the play *Candida*. And she, in turn, invited Mitzi and him to Oxford where she served as chairperson of the English department at the University there. She had told Jake that the writing program needed new life—one reason she was in Vermont—for ideas and a new faculty member. She strongly hinted there might be a place for him and a good salary if he were interested.

So, in June, after letters to and from Vella, Jake and Mitzi left Connecticut for a visit to Oxford, much to Mitzi's horror that Jake might even consider a move from their lovely home and friends in Old Greenwich to a small Southern town. "Just to look around," Jake had said. "You never know, a change, we might like it. We need a change, don't we? You know we haven't been getting along that great here. And if there's a position, and the money's better, we just might like all of it."

"Oh, God," Mitzi had said with a pained expression. And it was at Vella's home, during a gathering of English faculty, that Jake met her daughter Penelope. When he walked into Vella's living room, he hugged her, and his chin rested a long moment on her shoulder when his eyes connected with the dark-haired woman standing behind her. Jake was sure she was a foreigner, with that black hair framing a dark wide brow and curling lightly above eyes the color of a hurricane sea. And when she smiled at him, a wide full sensuous mouth said, "Well hello." Yes, he was staring, and yes he'd fallen in love right there on Vella's shoulder. He was embarrassed, and he had to catch his breath when Vella introduced Penelope because she'd taken everything he had in that one moment, his breath included.

"Oh, this is my daughter Penelope Warren," Vella said. "She teaches French at the W in Columbus and is visiting with me for a few weeks. Penelope, this is Jake and Mitzi Balfour from

Connecticut. We're hoping to snag Jake and make him part of our team here."

Jake was able to spend most of the evening talking to Penelope because Mitzi had suddenly come down with a major headache and had taken a cab back to the hotel. *"C'est la vie."* Jake thought it was uncanny the way Penelope liked all the same writers he did, tennis, biking; and he was very flattered by the way she responded to his every word. He was charmed by the way she teased him when she left the room, smiling back at him over her shoulder. He liked the way she held one glass of wine for most of the evening. Mitzi usually drank like a fish.

Jake was waiting for her to get back from the kitchen with more snacks when Vella introduced him to another faculty member. "Jake, I'd like you to meet Dr. Deborah Clancy, our infamous Miltonian scholar and Welty expert. She's quite versatile. I think you'll find her most interesting," Vella laughed. "This is Jake Balfour, Dr. Clancy. See if you can persuade him to fly south for the winter and add a little something to our humble college."

Jake sipped his drink, looking just above the rim of his glass and over Dr. Clancy's shoulder for Penelope, who seemed to be taking her time in the kitchen.

"Call me Deebo."

"Hmm?" Jake asked.

"Everybody calls me Deebo."

"Oh, I'm sorry. Okay. Deebo. So how do you like teaching here? Good atmosphere, the faculty and all? Seems to be," he said as he searched the room for Penelope.

"Oh no prob. It's great. But I need to warn you about something Jake, old boy."

"What?" he asked, only half-interested.

"Mrs. Penelope Warren."

"What do you mean?" Jake asked, suddenly annoyed.

"She's a spider. I mean like she chews up tall, blue-eyed boys like you and spits 'em out."

"Pardon?" Jake was getting angry.

"Her husband's a Baptist preacher over in Columbus, and she's not real happy with him, so she looks for ways to be happy. You know?"

"No! I don't know. And I don't like this conversation. Excuse me." Jake headed toward the bathroom. Deebo followed and stood outside the door.

"It's none of my business, Jake. But I saw her do this to

another boy, Dank, a CPA—taught accounting here. A good one. He finally took a job in Florida."

"Do what? Will you please leave me alone?"

"Okay, but you need to take that pretty wife of yours back up north and stay there."

There was a silence, and Jake thought she'd gone. She tapped her knuckles on the door. "She's a spider, Jake. She's a spider." Then she was gone.

Jake bumped into Penelope as he rounded the corner from the bathroom into the den. He studied her and held her gently for a moment so he could smell her hair, fresh and sweet. She pulled away after a minute and smiled at him. No poetry in the world could describe what he was feeling.

"I love your name. Penelope Warren. Penelope—I'd like to sing it."

"It's a silly name. It was my grandmother's and I got stuck with it—*n'est-ce pas?*"

"Well, then, I'll call you—Penn Warren."

"That's sillier."

"I guess, uh, I'm going to go now. See how Mitzi's doing. See you soon I hope."

"Yes, you will," Penelope said, as she held his eyes for one long moment, then gave him another slow, easy smile that made him warm inside.

When Jake got back to the hotel, Mitzi had decided she did not want to stay in Oxford, did not want to tour the campus, did not want to see Faulkner's home place, did not want to like any of it because she had no intention of becoming a southern belle. "Why don't you just stay here and play with Vella and her mousy daughter—what's her name?"

"Penelope. She's not mousy. I think she looks French. We've got a lot in common. You know, Grandad's being French. She knows a lot about the country and I just enjoyed . . . ."

"Oh bullshit! And your grandmother was German and I'm Italian and your mother . . . ."

"Don't talk about Mom."

"I was only going to say your mother had blue eyes. And what difference does any of it make? For God's sake, you've been screwy ever since your mother died. You're restless, can't settle. Maybe you're looking for a mother."

"Be quiet. *Just be quiet,*" Jake said slowly.

"No, I won't. I've tried to be patient. You've been depressed for over a year. Jesus Christ, Jake, other men's mothers have died."

Jake raised his hand to slap her.

"You just go ahead and do it."

He lowered his arm to his side and clenched his fist. "Go to sleep, Mitzi."

"I will. And I'm going home tomorrow. I can't stay here two days much less two weeks."

"But I promised them I'd give it a chance and look over the situation."

"Then you stay."

Mitzi turned out the light, and Jake tried to kiss her goodnight. She turned her face, leaving his lips to trail through her thick makeup into her stiff hair, frosted and frozen from too much spray.

And Jake did stay—for a month—because that's how long Penelope was to stay at Vella's. And he fell deeper and deeper in love with his dark-haired seductress, who would lie close to him while they picnicked at Lake Sardis, or who allowed him to put his arm around her waist while they strolled the Tallahatchee under a full moon, but who would not allow him to make love to her. For a while this just made him want her more, this elusive mystery lady who teased him with goodbye kisses—at first never fully on his mouth—but always close—just at the corner of his lips, or on the cheek, close to his ear.

And one afternoon, in the semi-dark of the university observatory, he almost shouted at her when he pulled her up to his face, so close he could feel her breath. "You have got to let me love you," he said, almost angry at first, and then with a pitiful plea, "please."

"Let me go, Jake. Don't force me. I can't now. Not while I'm still married to Phillip."

"When then?"

"I'm going to leave him. I've thought about it for a long time. I don't sleep with him, you know. I haven't for years. Soon. It'll be soon."

So Jake left it alone, satisfied with *what* he wasn't sure. He still had a wife to contend with. But he was content to spend the last few days on Penelope's terms, happy with the knowledge that she'd soon be free to love him. She seemed to love his compliments and advances. And he adored her. He'd stopped urging her to give into him because they were making love somewhere beyond the physical realm. They shared words, poetry, easy glances, and the sweetest kisses he would ever know. She would open her soft full lips just enough to warm him and give promise of a fire further in.

B.K Smith

He consumed her endearing remarks: "Jake, I want to write your hands. It bothers me when they reach to turn on a radio, or to build a fire. They should be only for poetry, for writing."

Jake ignored Deebo when he and Penelope left Vella's office on the last day of his stay. Penelope was to drive him to the airport, and they passed Deebo in the hallway. She just shook her head as Jake passed by. "So are you going to join us?" she asked.

"In a year. Got to fulfill some commitments first." Jake tossed the words back over his shoulder.

"Yeah, got to keep those commitments," Deebo said, folding her arms and falling back against the wall.

When Jake returned to Connecticut, his life with Mitzi, and life in general, seemed to get worse. His work suffered. All he could think about was writing to Penelope and getting her letters, which did not come very often. But, when they did, would hint at possibilities and tease him, would promise, but not fully commit to anything. He could not make love to Mitzi, and he knew their marriage was ending. He talked about a job in Oxford. She ignored him. By Christmas she asked him for a divorce. "I don't know what happened, Jake. I still love you. I just am not in love with you anymore." The months after that were a blur to Jake— in shock one moment—grieved to lose yet another love in his life— hopeful the next that when he moved to Oxford in the spring, things would be better. Penelope would be better. Penelope had promised to be divorced by summer, and in his obsessive stupor, Jake was ready to live happily ever after with the one true love of his life. He was unmarried before he knew it and listening to the bell ping above his head as the plane began to move, and he fastened his seatbelt for Mississippi.

II.

Jake awakened to the doorbell, but the arm across his forehead was still asleep. So was his left foot. He tried to get up to answer the door, but the tiny pins pricking his foot made it give way when he tried to walk. So he flopped back on the couch. It was only Deebo anyway, coming over to barbecue. Funny how Vella had assigned her the task of finding him an apartment, ironic how she'd been the only one to welcome him to Oxford for the summer. This overbearing, intrusive woman had been his neighbor for four months and his part-time bed partner for two. "It's open!" Jake yelled to the ceiling.

"Hey, J. R., time to get up, uncork the wine, put some music in the deck, and some steaks on the grill." Jake heard her plunk the meat in the refrigerator.

"Don't call me J. R.!" he grumbled as he massaged his foot.

"Want me to call you Jacques Raymond Balfour, like your granddaddy?"

"No! I hate that. Just call me Jake, *please*."

"Well, I let you call me Deebo instead of Deb-o-rah," she said as she slapped his thigh and edged her hips in against his side on the couch.

"Everybody calls you Deebo."

"I know."

"Where'd you get that name, anyway?" Jake asked.

"From my little brother, well, he's not so little anymore. He never could say Deborah until he was about six. It just stuck after that. I thought I'd already told you this. You never listen to me. I thought poets were supposed to listen, be real perceptive and stuff."

"Well, I'm not much of a poet these days."

"Sure you are. It'll come back to you. You've just had a lot on your mind—like me, right?" She laughed and poked at his ribs.

"Yeah, that's it," he muttered as he pulled the pillow from under his head and over his face.

"Oh you're so cute when you're sad—and shy and sleepy." She peeked under the pillow. "Just one blond curl almost falls into those big blue eyes." Deebo pulled the pillow away and tousled his hair. "How'd you get *Jake* from *Jacques* could I ask?"

"I was Jack all my life until I met Mitzi. She decided I'd be Jake, and *it stuck.*"

"God, let's open these curtains. It's so dark in here. You need some light and fresh air," she said as she opened the drapes and slid open the glass doors to the patio. "Oh, no wonder you're depressed. You've been trying to read that book again." She eyed *Revolutionary Road* on the table. "Why don't you try reading something light like *Titus Andronicus*? That'll lift your spirits right up. Yep, old Lavinia waving her bloody nubs around'll perk you right up." Deebo boxed at Jake's face.

"I like the book."

"Well, it depresses you and you can't finish it. Why can't you, anyway?" She sat on the floor next to the couch and rubbed his arm.

"I don't know."

B.K Smith

"Yeah, you do. Come on, 'fess up."

"I thought I told you, don't you listen?"

"Of course, I do, and you didn't. So spill it."

"Because I started reading it at Christmas. It was a gift from Richard."

"Richard?"

"Richard Yates. The guy who wrote it, *please*."

"Oh, sorry. You poets just read obscure stuff. How'm I supposed to know him? We scholars deal with the knowns."

"You mean you parasites."

"Don't start with that. I'll leave." She laughed.

"Promise?" he grinned.

"I wish you'd do that more often."

"What?"

"Smile. You're so much prettier," Deebo winked at him.

"Oh shut up."

"So why can't you finish it?" Deebo asked.

"Because I started reading it right after she asked me for the divorce."

"Mitzi?"

"No, Liz Taylor."

"Oh. That dead girl."

Jake knew she meant Mitzi. He'd told Deebo that the only way he could deal with the divorce was to pretend Mitzi was dead. "Yeah. Anyway, Mitzi was treating me like shit—after Christmas and through New Year's. She'd say she was going out. Just throwing it in my face—flaunting the fact that she was sleeping with that fruity squat of a hairdresser of hers. J-O-E-Y. She always said she felt so protected and proud when she was with me. How's he going to keep her safe?"

"Was he a fruit?"

"No, stupid, she was sleeping with him. Anyway she'd waltz right by me in her finest and announce that she was going out, and I'd be reading Richard's book and I'd have to stop. I just couldn't finish it. Still can't."

"God, that was cruel. But don't call me stupid."

"Right, and I had to put up with that until I could move here."

"Still hung up in that one place, huh? Still can't get those bricks laid, huh?" Deebo asked.

"Stones. It is a stone walkway."

"Whatever. Well, there's one thing that's sure to get laid," she said.

"What?"

"Me." Deebo grinned and ran her fingers down under Jake's jeans at the waist and eased out his T-shirt.

"I'm not in the mood." He tried to shift away from her hand.

"Oh you're always in the mood for me. You know that," she said as she slapped him on the stomach and began rubbing his skin under his shirt. "We need to get you some better reading material for now, like Welty's 'Why I Live at the P.O.' or 'Petrified Man'—reach in there and see if you can find me a cigarette without 'ny powder on it—thow your mind back if ya can, Leota, to yesterd'y. It's a scream. Idn't that funny?"

"Yeah, I guess," Jake mumbled.

"Oh, I know. You can read *Raney*."

"Who?"

"*Raney* by Clyde Edgerton. It's a scream. Southern writing at its best."

"I'm not into Southern."

"Well, you'd better get into Southern, boy, if you're gonna live here. That's what's wrong with you. Your North and South is turned around. You're upside down. We've got to get you acclimated, accustomed to the customs. You've got to feel that southern hospitality. It'll make you warm all over. And going to Antie and New Uncle Leo's tomorrow for Sunday dinner is a good place to start. You're still going aren't you?"

"I guess. Why do you call him New Uncle Leo?"

"Well, my cousin Reba's son, Harrison, started calling him that when Antie married again after Uncle Talmadge died. Harrison was only five and didn't understand why he had a new uncle, so the name just stuck. Everybody thought it was cute. Idn't that funny?"

"To everybody but Uncle Leo I'll bet," Jake said.

"You wanna back rub before we cook?" Deebo asked as she slowly rubbed Jake's stomach, letting her fingers slide in and out of his navel.

"No."

"God. That's a deep navel. You could hide quarters in there." She dug deeper into the stomach. "You really didn't wanna let go of your mama, did you?"

"No, I never did want to. I hate change, and death and being abandoned."

"Oh, I'm sorry I begot. I didn't mean to make you sad. But you've got me, and I'm not leaving."

Jake was a little hurt by her insensitivity and aggravated by her silly misuse of the language. She was always saying her "repartment" was dirty or something stupid.

"Reach in there and see if you can find me a quarter without 'ny lint on it, Leota," Deebo said as she tickled Jake's stomach.

He had to laugh. Sometimes he wanted to strangle Deebo. Other times, most of the time, she made him laugh and feel pretty good.

"See," she raised her shirt, "mine's real shallow. That's cause I'm adopted."

Jake laughed again. He knew Deebo was adopted, but it never seemed to bother her at all. He knew his hang-ups about abandonment concerned him much more than hers, if she had any.

"Let's drink some wine and cook," Deebo said as she kissed him quickly on the lips.

"Why'd you leave my front door open?" Jake asked as he got up and went to shut it.

"Well, Penny was right behind me. I thought he was coming in."

Jake rolled his eyes. He remembered the first night he'd met Deebo's fifteen-pound tomcat, Penny. It was his first night back in Oxford, before he'd gotten all his furniture. Deebo had made dinner for him. Penny kept getting in his lap, pricking his khaki pants with sharpened claws. Jake had been afraid to move at one point because Penny had zeroed in on his crotch, had dug the claws in and dared Jake to move as he purred and looked innocently across the table at Deebo.

"Why do you call this huge orange tom, this totally male animal, Penny?" Jake had asked.

"Well, when I got him, he was just a little old bitty thing. I started to name him Tiny cause all my cats growing up in Fulton were named Tiny—about nine of 'em. Hey, I didn't know Penny watn't a girl cat till he got big and grew balls. Then it was too late. He liked his name."

"Sorry I asked," Jake had said.

Jake shut the door and headed for the patio where Deebo was lighting the coals. "Love me, love my red-headed Kitty," Deebo said as she jabbed at Jake with a stick she'd used to spread the charcoal.

Jake sat out on the patio listening to the brittle buzz of a Mississippi August while Deebo went in and out to prepare the food. He wondered what Penelope was doing on this late summer's day. Deebo put her favorite cassette into the tape deck, turned it up loud, and brought Jake a glass of wine.

"Do you have to play that?" Jake shouted over the music.

"I love Tina Turner. I mean if I just had those long, sexy legs. Wouldn't you love it? 'I'll be thunder, you'll be lightning . . . . There'll be a storm one night and I will run to you for shelter.'"

She sang a little off key Jake thought.

Jake went inside and pushed the off button. "I don't want to listen to that. Let's just play the radio, not too loud, okay?"

"Oh, I begot. That song makes you think of that big-nosed woman, doesn't it?"

"She doesn't have a big nose," Jake answered defensively.

"Why she looks like a broad-nosed African to me, just a broad-nosed . . ."

"That's enough," Jake said firmly but quietly, staring hard at Deebo's rather large pugged nose. "I think she's pretty."

"Infatuation is blind. Have you heard from Pen-A-lope?"

"She calls sometimes on Sunday when he's out visiting sick people or whatever."

"When on Sunday?"

"A couple of weeks ago, maybe three," Jake said.

"Been rough since old Phil found the letters you wrote back in June, huh? What'd you write in those letters anyway, to get him so mad? Love poems and stuff?"

"He had no right to read my letters to her."

"He's married *to her*," Deebo retorted.

"They were none of his business. And some minister, some Christian he is, calling me a son-of-a-bitch and threatening me if I ever came near her again. Said he was responsible for protecting his family."

"From the shady likes of you, huh?" Deebo smiled. "Have you seen her?"

"Not since early July when I drove over to Columbus and surprised her after a class. We took a walk in the park, but she was so nervous, looking around and over her shoulder, I left. She's just scared. Handling it the best way she knows how."

"So, you can't get near her. He won't let you, huh? What a convenient excuse."

"It's no excuse. She's working it out. I mean what would you do if your husband threatened to take your child away from you?"

"He said that?"

"He was going to take Jeremy out of summer camp and move out, divorce her. I mean, I couldn't let her lose her only son over this. Could I?"

"No, I guess not." Deebo slapped the raw steaks down on the hot grill top. Jake detected some anger in her movements. Her mood seemed to be sizzling along with the fresh steaks.

"I'm sorry. Maybe we shouldn't talk about this," he said, genuinely apologetic.

"No. I started it. So I guess I'm just your whore, huh? Your bed buddy every other weekend or so?"

Jake looked shocked. "No. Honest. I care about you, Deebo. You saved my life."

Deebo broke into song, "Jesus save your pie for me. . . ."

"What's that?"

"That's one of those songs we'll be singing if we go to church with Antie and New Uncle Leo tomorrow."

"That's really a song?" Jake asked.

"Well it's actually called 'Jesus, Saviour, Pilot Me.' But when I was a kid, I heard it the other way and that's the way I sang it."

Jake laughed, but stopped short and turned his smile to a frown when Penny came bounding around the corner chasing a lizard.

"Don't let him get my lizard!" Jake shouted and moved toward the cat.

"Are you serious?" Deebo asked as Jake relaxed back in his lounge chair. The lizard was perched safely in a crack half way up the brick wall. Jake could tell he was scared as he blew his pink throat in and out. The cat jumped for him but couldn't reach. "It's just a lizard, Jake. You know, cats like to chase 'em and all." Deebo sipped her wine and sat in the chair next to Jake.

"Yes, but he's mine. I saved his life the other day."

"How?"

"He'd crawled into an empty flower pot on the table there. I looked inside it, thought about throwing it away or maybe planting something in it, and I saw him. I only saw his body, tail up, and couldn't figure out what was wrong. He'd gotten his head wedged in the hole at the bottom and couldn't get it unstuck. I picked up the pot, looked underneath, and stared at him. There was this pained expression on his face."

Deebo laughed and held her stomach. "That's a scream."

"No, it wasn't funny really. I knew exactly how he felt —his body trapped one place, his head in another. He was helpless."

"How'd you get him out?" Deebo said, trying to stifle a giggle.

"Well, I pushed at his nose with my finger, but that must've hurt or irritated his neck because when I looked inside the pot at his other half, he was really wiggling."

"What'd you do?"

"Well, I figured I'd get my hammer and crack open the pot and get him out. So I set the pot down on the table to run get the hammer, and I winced really hard because I just knew I'd smashed his head." By then, Jake was laughing too. "But luckily I'd gotten him on just the right spot of the lattice work and he was okay."

"So did you get him out?"

"Yeah. I cracked it open and he sat there for a minute—stunned I guess, from the hammer, and his neck was cut a little on the side. After a minute or two he scooted off."

"So now he's *your* lizard."

"Yeah. I saved his life. Now I'm responsible for him."

"Ja-ake, methinks that only applies to people. He's just a green, sometimes brown, lizard. Get a grip, boy. What's his name?"

"I don't know."

"See, you don't even know his name. How important can he be?" Deebo sat back in her chair. Penny sat patiently, never taking his eyes away, swishing his tail slowly back and forth across the patio.

"Well, I call him Charlemagne sometimes or Alexander."

"Alexander Salamander," Deebo laughed.

"Or, Bubblegum," Jake said, "when he blows his throat in and out like that. Looks like he's turning brown."

Deebo rolled her eyes at Jake. "So how do you know it's the same one you rescued?"

Jake got up from his chair to point out the small nick on the lizard's neck and when he did, it dropped from the wall to Penny. Jake tried to grab the cat, but he was too late. Penny had severed the lizard's tail from its body.

"Do something with your damned cat. He's killing him!" Jake shouted.

"Oh, hold your water, Jake," she said as she picked up Penny and held him tight so the lizard could waddle away like a miniature crocodile. He disappeared into a drainpipe. Jake was relieved, but he stared at the tail as it continued to wiggle on the patio. "Hey, it's okay, Jake. They grow 'em back. No sweat."

"They do? Their tails?"

"Yeah, it's a fact. Neat trick, huh? Let's eat." She dropped Penny from her lap and went inside to get a plate for the steaks.

"I love Emmylou, don't you?" Deebo asked as she cut a chunk of her steak and tossed it to Penny.

"Who?" Jake asked as he reached across the patio table for the salad.

"Emmylou Harris—on the radio—if I could only win your love," Deebo broke into song.

"I don't like country music." Jake looked down and snarled at Penny who didn't flinch.

"Oh don't be so hard on Penny. He's a pretty good Kitty."

"Kitty? That makes me think of a small animal, one that doesn't search out and destroy everything in its path."

"Well, he's really only gone through one bad kitty stage in his life," Deebo said as she tossed the cat more steak.

"When?"

"When he was younger. I took him home to Mama and Daddy's for Christmas vacation a couple of years ago."

"Yeah?"

"Well, they had a zoo there anyway—Marco the dog, Betty and Bob parakeets, Charley the cat, Henry the turtle, and Fish. I think it kinda made Penny nervous, all those animals. So he just took it upon himself to reduce the number—you know, population control."

"What happened?" Jake asked as he finished his dinner and balled up his napkin to throw at Penny.

"The first day, we'd gone out to eat lunch, and when we got back, we found Fish lying on the coffee table. Penny had apparently just reached in the bowl, pulled him out and left him to flop and die. We thought he'd done the same to Henry cause we couldn't find him. Then we saw one little turtle foot underneath a huge shell in the fish bowl. Penny had turned that over on him and killed him too. Then the next day . . ."

"There's more?"

"Yeah. Penny jumped up on the bird cage, hung by his claws, and scared Betty and Bob to death. Bob, literally, he died of a heart attack."

Jake laughed. "Hey, I'm sorry."

"That's okay." Deebo was laughing too. "The funny part was Mama. She's so understated about everything. She looked at me and said, "Well, I guess we ought to let Penny get out more, huh?" And I cracked up. "Idn't that funny?"

"Yeah," Jake chuckled.

"Hey, let's go shopping tonight, at the malt?"

"The what?"

"That's what Antie calls the mall. She says, 'Let's go over to Gaythers at the malt.' Idn't that a scream? Wait till you meet her."

"I can't wait," Jake said as he cleared the table.

"Hmm watn't it all belicious?"

"Do you have to do that?" Jake moaned a little, but he consented to go shopping in Tupelo with Deebo.

III.

They walked through the mall later, looking into shop windows and stopping in a few stores to browse. "This is my favorite place," Deebo said, pointing into a jewelry store. "It would be dangerous for me to go in there."

"Where's all your jewelry anyway?" he asked. "All those expensive rings your parents gave you?"

"I hocked them."

"What! What for?"

"I needed the cash."

"That's stupid."

"Don't ever call me stupid!"

"Well, it . . ."

"Don't ever. Besides I can buy 'em back within ninety days. Forget it. What's your favorite store?"

"It's not here."

"Well, what is it?"

"It's called *The Sock Market.* I love socks. You can buy me 20 pairs of socks for my birthday, and I'll be happy."

"Now that's stupid," Deebo laughed. "Hey, there's Felicia Bane," she said. "You gotta meet this chick. She was in one of my classes last term. She's a scream." Felicia, a tall young black girl, stood next to a shorter young black man. They were looking at lingerie in a store window.

"Felicia," Deebo said.

"Well, hey, Docta Clancy. What's shakin'?"

"Felicia, this is a friend of mine I wanted to meet you—Jake Balfour. Jake, this is Felicia Bane, one of my star students," she laughed.

"Yeah, you bet, doc. Hey, Jake, glad to make your acquaintance."

"Yeah, me too," Jake nodded.

"Oh, this is my boyfriend Norman." She jabbed the young man beside her. "Speak, Norman."

"Hello, glad to meet you," he said shyly.

"Well, we gotta run get some yogurt before everything closes. See you Felicia, Norman." Deebo said.

"Bye too," Felicia answered. "Ya'll be good now."

"Idn't she funny, Jake?"

"Yeah. 'Speak Norman.'" Jake laughed.

"I was giving a lecture on Pantheism one day last term, and she just stands up in the middle of class and says, 'I believe in Jesus Christ of Nazareth, and he wouldn't like this. No sir. Ya'll gonna burn in the piss 'a hell. And it's tyne ta go.' And she points to her watch, 'Tyne ta go.' Idn't that funny?"

"Yeah." Jake chuckled.

"And another time one of the little sorority Sues—probably Mary Margaret Ashland, a Kappa Kappa Gamma from Huntsville—threw-up in class. Probably partied too hard the night before. And Felicia gets up disgusted, and says, 'Oooh, I'm leavin'. I mean she didn't even pre-warn, that is, let us know. Tyne ta go.' Idn't that a scream?"

Sometimes Jake just couldn't laugh at all of Deebo's corny jokes, but that was a good one, he thought, and he roared. His sister had told him he needed to laugh more, and Deebo certainly helped him to meet that need.

Jake and Deebo grabbed some yogurt and then headed back to his apartment for the night. Her place was always messier than his, so he liked to spend the night at home. They lay on the carpet listening to the low tones of a Kitaro tape, and Deebo read to him from *Raney*—a scene in the K&W Restaurant. He loved it.

"That's to prepare you for Antie's lunch tomorrow," Deebo laughed.

She was always reading to Jake. He loved listening to her. She read and taught her classes in a more sophisticated voice than the one she projected at home, that down-home southern girl voice. He liked this one.

"Why don't you ever read to me?" she asked. "Don't you have some poetry you could read to me?"

"Well, I did write one a couple of weeks ago. But I don't think you'd want to hear it."

"Why? Is it about Pen-a-lope? Try me."

Jake pulled it out of a book on the bottom of his bookshelf and sat on the carpet. Deebo lay down beside him and propped on her elbow to listen.

"It's called 'Quicksilver,'" Jake said as he began to read.

I am Urthona. You are Oothoon.
I wish that were true.
But you, dear, are Thel,
closing the book on
generations of lush
green rebellion.
You step lightly, asking
the clod to forgive you
again and again.
And you slide like quicksilver
back into the garden light
of Beulah when
the pebbles of passion and life
bruise your tender foot.
Your soul is bound there,
entangled with the dark root,
so we can't tell the
difference.
But on a day,
the moonlit forest will
provide no places to hide,
no stone unturned, as you
break the Bromion
bonds and fly,
silver pearls streaking
from your wings
as you envelope

another in the
golden light
of Eden.

"Hmm. Let's see now," Deebo said, "I recognize Oothoon. She's a William Blake character who gets raped by Bromion, and he chains her to him until she gets away, right?"

"That's close." Jake smiled.

"But I don't know Thel and Urthona. Are they Blake characters, too?"

"Blake sometimes referred to the imagination as Urthona. And Thel refuses to step foot in the state of generation. It's too filled with life, passion, and uncertainties. She prefers the safe

B.K Smith

quiet of Beulah."

"So let me take a wild guess," Deebo said, "Oothoon and Thel are a combination of Miss Priss Penelope here, am I right?"

"It's just a poem," Jake said, not raising his eyes, and returning the poem to the book.

"Oh, don't worry. I'm not gonna hassle you. It's actually pretty good."

"You're good," Jake said.

"What?"

"I mean you're good. I listened to you teach a few weeks ago."

"You did."

"I was over visiting Vella and cleaning up my new office for fall term, and I stopped by your room. You were doing Milton's 'Sonnet 19,' and some other works, but that one really hit me. 'They also serve who only stand and wait.' You did a good job with it."

"Well, thanks. That means a lot coming from you. And speaking of coming from you." Deebo pulled Jake down for a kiss. He loved making love to her. She was always totally uninhibited. She gave him everything and always surrendered her body completely, holding nothing back. He got up to cut off the lamp and returned to her on the floor. "It's like moonlight, isn't it?" he asked.

"What?"

"The light from the stereo?"

"Hmm," she mumbled as she pulled him closer, the pale green light bathing them and the room where they made love. Later Jake took her to bed and snuggled in under her chin like he used to do with Mitzi. It made him feel secure.

IV.

At eight o'clock Jake awakened to the sound of Deebo brushing her teeth. He was in a foul mood as he watched her in the bathroom mirror. He hated the way she never washed the toothpaste out of her mouth, and he wouldn't let her kiss him until she did.

"Wash your mouth out before you try to kiss me."

"And who says I want to?" Deebo wiggled her hips at him.

"You know, you're built like a little stump." Jake was sorry he'd said that.

"You can't make me mad, Jake, can't hurt my feelings," she said as she jumped on top of him. "I know I'm plain, regular brown hair, pugged nose, squatty body—but I put out, don't I? That girl, that girl over in Columbus, she don't put out, does she?"

Jake tried not to laugh, but failed, as usual. When she wanted a smile from him, she generally got it.

"And you aren't going to get outa taking me to Antie's for Sunday lunch. So get packin'. We'll be tree and tree stump. How 'bout that? So there."

"I'm not going to church," Jake snorted.

"Fine. Fine. Just get up and at 'em. It's two hours to Jackson. I've got to go feed Penny and find a dress to wear. Bye now. Don't you go back to sleep."

Jake turned over and did just that. His sister called from Connecticut at 8:30.

"Hi babes. How's the South treating you?"

"Lousy," he snarled.

"What's wrong? Tell your big sis the problem."

"Oh nothing. I'm just in a bad mood. Actually everything's okay."

"Just okay, huh? Have you seen Penelope?"

"No, the bastard's keeping her from me."

"Really. Seems to me she'd be with you if that's what she really wanted."

"Extenuating circumstances," he yawned.

"Uh, huh. Late night? Where's Deebo? I like what I've heard about her."

"Next door getting ready to take me to the last Southern supper at *Antie's*, her aunt's, for lunch."

"How are you two doing?"

"I swear, Sis, sometimes I can't stand her. She acts so dumb. She hocks her jewelry for cash, and she flushes the toilet while she's taking a leak."

"Maybe she took cash for her jewelry so she could buy you a nice birthday present next week. Ever think of that?"

"No."

"What's really wrong, Jake?"

"She's just not pretty! I can't help it. She's just not."

"Is she cute?"

"No, well sometimes, like when she's being Magnolia, who's just got to have a box fan out by thuh poowul befoa the woah."

"You like her, but you're mad at her because she's not pretty. That right?"

"Sort of."

"Well, you know where the last pretty package got you. That's

B.K Smith

not everything, Jake. Seems like she loves you and is really good for you."

"But I still love Penelope," he whined.

"Oh, you've been with her a total of four weeks out of your life."

"Sometimes she can make me mad just brushing her teeth."

"Who?"

"Deebo. And other times, she can't do anything wrong. And she's the best I've ever had in bed."

"Shame on you, Jake. Well, sounds like there are all these women in your life who aren't in your life. Maybe you won't let them be."

"I tried with Penelope. I wanted her."

"Oh, she doesn't deserve you anyway. Listen, Desperado, you'd better let somebody love you before it's too late. Deebo's got my vote."

"How's Dad?"

"Oh, fine. He's dating *some* woman. I guess she's okay."

"Tell him I'll be home for Christmas." They both laughed. "And don't worry. I'm fine. Just grumpy this morning."

"You think I don't know you by now, little brother?"

"Thanks for calling, Sis."

"You bet. Love you."

"Love you too."

Jake was off the phone, showered and dressed by the time Deebo rang the doorbell just before ten o'clock. "Well, I hope you're in a better mood, lovah," she ribbed him. "I guess we just ought to let you out more, huh?"

"I'm fine. My sister called," he said as he unlocked the car door for Deebo.

"What'd she have to say?"

Jake walked around to the driver's side and slid in. "She said she likes you."

"She doesn't even know me."

"She likes what she hears," Jake said.

"And you, do you like me?" Deebo eased her dress up mid-thigh.

"You look nice."

"You look nice, he says. I'm dressed to the nines and he says I look nice."

Jake chuckled and headed the car out of the parking lot and toward Jackson.

"Let me pre-warn you about two things," Deebo said, as they pulled into her aunt's driveway later.

"What's that?"

"Don't try to put any dishes in the dishwasher, and don't be too put off by Antie's continual attributions to Uncle Talmadge."

"He's dead isn't he?" Jake asked.

"Yeah, but according to Antie, he knew everything that was gonna happen in the world and the hereafter three days before he died. You'll see."

"What's wrong with the dishwasher?"

"Nothing, but she won't use it. Now you might find a hairbrush or some face powder in there, but no dishes. She likes to handwash 'em. I couldn't find my hairbrush once when I stayed over, and my cousin Reba told me to look in Antie's dishwasher. There it was, sittin' pretty in the rack, along with some combs and a scarf or two."

"That's weird," Jake said as they walked to the door. Lunch was ready, so Deebo quickly introduced Jake to her cousin Reba, her son Harrison, Antie's daughter Lou and her husband Sanford, Antie, and New Uncle Leo.

"Mama was about to give up on ya'll," Lou said as she offered Jake a platter of fried chicken. "You like chicken, don't you, Jake?"

"Uh, yes, I do, thanks."

"He mighta rather have the pot roast," Antie said. "Do ya son?" she asked.

"No, this is great."

"Antie's homemade mash potatoes are the best in Jackson, Jake. Try these," Reba said as she passed him the bowl.

"Thanks. I love *mashed* potatoes."

"Slap a few of these on your plate, Jake," Sanford said as he forked three breaded disks onto Jake's plate. Jake thought they looked a lot like green and brown wheels stacked next to his potatoes. And he thought Sanford looked like an over-sized nose guard for the Giants.

Jake looked to Deebo for answers to the last three items of food "slapped" on his plate. "Oh, Antie's fried green *tomatoes* are the best in Jackson, too," Deebo said with a grin and an emphasis on tomatoes.

Jake suddenly imagined his stomach trying to process all the fried delicacies as first one person offered him fried squash, another fried okra, and another cornbread. Jake looked at his plate when everyone had finally stopped passing things and had settled in to

45   *B.K Smith*

eat them. Mitzi wouldn't have liked that plate, he thought. It was a mound of dull green and brown, not the color-coordinated meals of rigattoni or lasagna or exotic salads, or bright green parsley sprinkled around a plate of turkey, golden candied yams, and deep red cranberry sauce. There was definitely no color there. But Jake ate anyway, carefully.

He noticed that Harrison was tearing at a chicken leg like it was the last food he'd ever eat, and Jake felt that maybe he was wrong to cut his chicken breast with the knife and fork. Reba misread Jake's dilemma. She slapped Harrison's arm, and the leg dangled from the side of his mouth, still firmly secure in the grasp of his teeth. "Have some manners, Harrison, with Sunday company," she scolded, and nodded toward Jake.

Jake tried to fix it and make the boy feel better. "So you're Harrison, huh? That's a strong name. You look really . . ."

Antie cut Jake off. "Reba found that name in a book over to the junior college when she went there. It was about a boy named Burt Vongut."

"No, Antie, it was about a boy named Harrison Bergeron, *written* by Kurt Vonnegut," Reba said proudly. "I took English at night, but I had to quit, but I'm gonna go back, soon as we can get back on our feet."

"Oh, that's great," Jake said. "What does your husband do?" he asked. Deebo kicked him under the table before the silence began. Sanford looked at Lou, Lou at Deebo.

"Why, he don't do nothin' since he hooked up with that floozy Maybelle Kitchens," Antie snorted.

Jake knew he'd asked the wrong thing, and was thankful when Deebo rescued him. "Did ya'll see that special on T.V. the other night about the ozone layer disappearing?"

"Yeah," Sanford said, "we saw it. Looks like the sun's gonna fry us like an egg if we ain't more careful."

"Talmadge said that three days 'fore he died," Antie piped in. Jake heard Uncle Leo choke on his tea. "I heard we needed to plant more trees," Reba added.

"Why, your Uncle Talmadge planted some right out there 'fore he died," Antie said. "He knew to." Lou shivered in her chair, "It all scares me to death. I read where there was gonna be more tornadoes and hurricuns in the next five years cause a some. . ."

Antie interrupted again, "Talmadge said the very same words three days 'fore he died."

"Mama, hush!" Lou shouted. "You know good 'n well Daddy

was in a coma two weeks *before he died*." Everyone was silent again. "Now," Lou added.

"Well it mighta been two weeks, but he said it," Antie insisted as she began to clear the table of plates, slamming each one down hard as she stacked them. Jake thought they might break.

"Ya'll want some duzzert?" Antie asked, daring anyone to say yes.

"Not me, boy, I'm full as a hog," Sanford patted his stomach. Jake agreed with him on that one, but didn't say it.

"I do, Antie," Harrison piped.

"Oh, you ate like a horse, boy. Go thow some baseball with Sanford," Reba said.

"Okay."

"Nuh, Nuh. I got a settle a little on the porch first."

"Come on I'll toss some with you," Jake said as he patted Harrison on the shoulder.

"I'll go with you," Uncle Leo said, startling Jake. He wasn't sure before that moment if the shy, balding little man could speak.

"We'll help Antie clean up," Deebo said as she guided Jake out the back door behind Uncle Leo and Harrison.

"Wait'll you see New Uncle Leo's fast ball. He's got a mean fast ball," Harrison yelled as he jumped off the back porch to the grass.

"So much for southern hospitality, huh Jake? I'm really sorry," Deebo said sheepishly. "Paradise lost, huh?" she giggled.

"Hey, no prob. I'm gonna thow some baseball," Jake laughed and went on out.

"Let's get that Wal-Mart shopper after the dishes, Antie," Deebo said as she walked back into the kitchen. "There's always some good buys in there."

Jake figured everything was okay inside by the time they tired of pitching. He'd heard Antie exclaim, "Oohwee, if I had a million dollars, my feet wouldn't touch the ground 'til I got to Wal-Mart. Why you can't see it all, much less buy it." He knew all was fine when Antie kept trying to give food to Deebo and him to take home with them. "Why, I'll just hafta pitch it out if you don't," she said as they headed for the door.

Jake didn't mind it at all when Antie squeezed him goodbye and then Reba and Lou, or when Sanford slapped him on the back. Uncle Leo just shook his hand, and Harrison gave him a shy grin. Southern hospitality.

He and Deebo had a good time on the way back to Oxford,

B.K Smith

talking about the Sunday dinner. "How'd you like it?" Deebo asked.

"Why, I couldn't take it all in," Jake kidded. "I really like your *Uncle Leo*. He talked to me about his paint business and how he misses it. He seems kinda lonesome for his work, mixin' new colors, and mixin' with people."

"God, you're sounding like a Southern boy—in just one day," Deebo laughed.

"That's a fact, ma'am."

Deebo flipped on the radio and snuggled in under Jake's arm when they were halfway to Oxford. A light rain was hitting the windshield.

"I'm a little sleepy."

"Well, you just go right to sleep," Jake said as he reached to turn off the radio.

"No, I love that song. Listen. That's Anne Murray. 'It's only desire, not yet a fire, let's keep it that way. . . Hmm . . . we forget we're not cheaters yet, let's keep it that way.' Idn't that pretty?"

"It sure is."

"And you didn't like country music," Deebo said as she fell asleep against Jake.

"I like that one," Jake said thoughtfully.

"Hmm, I love you too," Deebo mumbled.

V.

Rain was coming down hard when they reached Oxford at five o'clock. Deebo headed toward her apartment to change and to feed Penny, and promised Jake she'd be over soon. "Maybe we'll take a shower together while it showers," she giggled as she ran into her apartment.

Jake's phone was ringing when he got inside. He grabbed it and said, "Hello."

"Jake?"

He knew the voice, and his own voice weakened as his breath caught in his throat. "Penny?" he coughed a little. "Is that really you?"

"Please don't call me that name. I hate it. You know Phillip calls me that."

"I'm sorry. I don't know what made me say it. I hate it too. There's this cat . . ."

"I can't talk long, Jake. I don't have much time. Are you okay?"

"Yeah. I'm fine," he lied. He was shaking like a leaf.

"How's everything with Phillip?" Jake couldn't understand why he was so cold suddenly. He reached into the closet and grabbed an old blanket that he and Deebo had taken to the Tallahatchee. She loved to go there to feed her "orphan river kits." Jake wasn't hearing everything Penelope was saying. His head was swimming. Maybe he was coming down with something.

"Well my *partner* thinks we can make it a little longer," she said, and Jake wrapped himself tighter in the blanket. He thought about the mama cat and her kittens they'd found on the Fourth of July. Deebo had wanted to bring them home.

"No hope for us, huh?" he asked.

"I don't know, Jake. I've lived in this cast-iron pot for so long. I just don't know how to get out."

Jake wondered if the mama cat and her kittens were out of the rain.

"Maybe I just need more time. Jake, are you there? Is it raining there?"

"Yes. It's pouring." They'd been abandoned at the river. He wished they'd brought them home. They were probably starving.

"It sounds so good on the roof—it's so soft against my window. Are you watching it, Jake? I wish you were stretched out here beside me. We could listen very carefully, and hear it tapping the roses in the garden. It's warm in here. I'm unbuttoning the white silk blouse you love, lower and lower, open for your hands, your poetry. Can you smell the roses, Jake? Touch them in your mind."

The chill had completely frozen his outer body. It had gone deeper and deeper into the core of him, around his heart. It was freezing his heart.

"Hmm. My bed's so soft and this rain is just . . ."

Jake threw the phone across the room. "Siren!" he yelled. "Spider! Bitch!"

Jake sat on the floor, pushed a cassette into the tape deck and stared at the green light from the stereo. He began to daydream inside his blanket, pulled it up around his ears, trying to shut out the buzz from the telephone. He wasn't sure how long he'd sat there before Deebo walked in.

"What are you doing in that blanket, chief? It's 80 degrees outside—Prince Funny Feather." She pulled it back from his face. "I thought you didn't want to hear that song. Jake? Speak, Jake," she laughed, and then she saw the telephone receiver under the stereo. "Oh, God, she called you, didn't she? Damnit, I only left you alone for 30 minutes. I knew I heard that phone ringing. She called, didn't she? Damnit, talk to me!"

"I have these fantasies," Jake said finally as he eased the blanket from around his shoulders. "And I don't want to anymore."

"What fantasies?" Deebo asked as she sat facing him.

"It's raining, see, and she comes to my door. I look out the window, and I see her standing there in an overcoat or raincoat or something like that. And this song is playing."

"'Thunder and Lightning,' right?" Deebo asked.

"Uh-huh, and I ask, 'Who is it?' She answers, 'Lightning,' and she laughs. Then I let her in. We both laugh, but she puts her arms around my neck and lets me slide my hands inside her coat. She doesn't have anything on underneath, and I make love to her. See, listen to the end of the song—'no betrayal, no denial, no need to explain. We'll collide.'" Jake cupped his face with his hands and shook his head. "God, I've never been so embarrassed. I'm stupid! Call me stupid."

"No, I won't. Just caught you at a weak moment, that's all."

"I'm crazy. I used to be so confident and cocky. When I was Jack, when my mother was alive, making love to Mitzi, my work. I'm just losing it, I tell you. I'm crazy! Tell me I'm crazy!" Jake peeked through his fingers. He saw a tear easing its way down Deebo's cheek.

"No, you're not crazy," she said quietly. "You're just not over them yet, any of them. But, you'll be okay. You'll get it back." She took Jake's hands from his face. "Come on. I'll read to you. And then we'll do carpet swirls and make love in the moonlight of the radio dial." She got up, moved over to the coffee table, and reached for *Revolutionary Road*.

FULL CIRCLE

Last night the moon was a quarter slice. This made Tess uneasy as she tried to sleep. She longed for the lunar pull that seemed to balance her responsive centers when the moon filled up full circle with a luminous lotion. She longed for the order it provided in her life, making everything fit into its proper place—picture perfect. But all she could see through the narrow slit between the bedroom curtains was a tiny sliver of natural moonlight, hanging in the sky just a few inches higher, it seemed, than the harsh, artificial beam from the street lamp outside. She tossed and turned, flipping like a decked fish; at least that's what her fiance, Coy, had called her earlier in the night when she had awakened him with her erratic movements beneath the sheets and on top of the comforter.

Tess continued to shift positions in the bed. She tried sleeping on her back, her side, even crouched on her knees and elbows, with her backside in the air as she'd done as a child. She tried sitting up, crossing her legs, pretending to know the secrets of yoga and meditation—taking deep breaths and repeating strange words over and over again—"Neecheemoo" or "Yatsinblak"—in hopes this would relax her. Nothing worked. She decided to slide under the covers, next to Coy's back, and *spoon*, as he'd called it. She pressed her cool breasts against his back and let the length of her body merge with the shape of his. This was good for a few moments, until Tess became restless again. She closed her eyes and began to press harder and harder toward sleep. She dug her knees deeper and deeper into the bends of Coy's legs, and she pressed her pelvis hard into his hips and thighs until she woke him up and he reacted.

"Cripes, Tess, you're squeezing me to death. Would you let me sleep."

"Jerk," she mumbled, as she lay there watching him return to his sleep. She felt resentful. He was selfish. He could've held her in his arms and rubbed her back—put her to sleep. Tess stared at Coy's back, the mole on his neck, the small canyon that ran between his ear and head. She stuck her tongue out at him and flopped on her back, pulling the sheet over her head. She pretended she was dead. She held her breath for a long while and folded her hands on her chest. Maybe that would make him happy, she thought.

Tess lay still, listening to her heart beat in her ears and in her

B.K Smith

throat. She was aware of every fiber in her body and every inch of skin and hair on the surface. She ran her hands across her face, her breasts, her abdomen, down to the soft cushion of hair between her thighs. She bent her legs and drew them to her chest, caressed the roundness of her knees, and then slid her fingers across her ankles, and to her feet where she grasped her toes, counting each one slowly. Tess was afraid. She knew she wasn't suffering from a simple case of insomnia. She knew the sickness had returned— the shapeless intruder that attacked her central nervous system from time to time. She closed her eyes and imagined it creeping in under her left anklebone, filtering through knee tendons, sleeping for awhile in her hip socket, climbing rib rungs, and perching on her shoulder blade before sliding in under the base of her skull. She felt it hit, seizing the center of her brain. Her body twitched for a moment while the natural antibodies were knocked off one by one. Tess opened her eyes. They clouded. It was like staring through a haze of tanning oil that seeps into the eyes while sunbathing.

Tess knew it was beginning again—the problem she'd had since she was just a girl. She had called it by technical names, such as depression, and by less formal names, such as "the funk" or "the blues." But none of those could describe it. It was a plunge into deepest despair and bewilderment. And once there, the place was dark and dank and lonely. Tess lay still, twisting the edge of the sheet into a knot, and taking short, quick breaths almost to the point of hyperventilating. She would give the sickness a real name—not a plunge into despair, but blunge. And not into the dark depths, but into the dank. *Blungedank.* Yes, it would have a name—that force that entered her body and mind with no ordinary warning, no tangible signs like sneezing or fever. It was usually upon her before she could make any preparations— sneaking into the recesses of her body through various skin points. The symptoms were tricky, seldom taking the same form. Most often it happened after a full moon, when Tess felt her corpuscles and blood lanes degravitate, and felt her skin stretch to an almost unbearable tautness, causing bruises to appear near joints where the skin was pressed tight over bones. Usually, it happened after the brief period of one or two days when her life was completely in order—when red lights always changed to green; when strangers on elevators smiled and spoke because Tess was so irresistibly charming; when orgasm was guaranteed with Coy and he begged for more lovemaking, because she was so hot in bed on those nights; when bills were usually less than anticipated. Life was good for Tess when the moon was bright and full. But when it began to wane, so did the order in Tess's life, and she was left vulnerable to the sickness—the newly dubbed *Blungedank*.

Tess awoke the next morning, tired and sore from her fitful night. She heard gargling sounds from the bathroom, and propped on her elbow to watch Coy prepare for the day. First, he would brush his teeth, leaving the cap off the toothpaste and stuck to the Formica; then he would shave, leaving stubborn little hairs scattered all over the sink for her to clean away. The same pattern every day. Her eyes traveled over his stocky body—built like a stump, she thought. She wondered why everyone thought he was such a catch, with his huge, brown cow eyes, much too large for his face, and his curly dark hair that never stayed in place. Her mother was the worst, claiming that he was such a nice young man, so polite, such nice manners. If her mother only knew how disgusting he could be, leaving his dirty socks all over the apartment, or singing off-key monotones in the shower. If her mother only knew he was shacking up with her daughter.

Tess realized that the dank was beginning its course, but not like with the flu or a simple virus, she would have to endure its four miserable phases before it was finished with her. And the first phase was total obsession with small details and annoyances. Coy always accelerated the first stage at an alarming rate.

As Coy finished in the bathroom, Tess buried her face in her pillow, pretending to sleep. The Emporium where she worked was closed for repairs. Vandals had broken the front windows, destroyed the displays, and had stolen some valuable art objects. Tess could sleep in for the day, so she knew Coy wouldn't bug her to get up. He would go on to his classes, and then to his assistant's job in the phys-ed department at the university, and would leave her alone for the day.

Tess stayed in bed until eleven o'clock, counting small squares in the ceiling and multiplying them by different numbers. She counted the books in the bookshelf—one hundred five—she finally concluded. When she did get up, she crouched in one corner of the sofa, staring at the ancient African mask on the wall. She mimicked the face, grimacing, and forced her forefingers into the corners of her mouth to stretch her lips wide across her teeth. Tess tired of the gestures and decided to light some candles, lots of them. The blue ones would calm her. She switched off the light, closed the curtains, and watched the flickers of light dance in the

B.K Smith

room. She enjoyed the shapes and rhythms, like black cat clouds drifting across a full moon.

Tess listened to the unsteady thump and pop of a tennis ball on the court outside the apartment building. She looked at the clock. She had lost two hours somewhere. She had to get up, keep moving, change her point of interest. Her attention span for minute details was all-consuming. She extinguished the candles one by one, speaking softly to each dying flame. She turned on a box fan to clear the room of smoke and enjoyed the drone and whine of the propeller as she changed the dial from high to low and back to high. It seemed to pull her in and out like a kaleidoscope.

Tess switched on the T.V. and concentrated on the slow loop of the picture emerging, the expanding sound. She listened carefully to the soap opera characters—to their problems, to their pronunciation—sibilant sounds, illegitimate children, guttural enunciations, prodigal sons, loud and soft voices, lovers and languages. Then Tess listened intently to a commercial about cake mixes. They say that consumers want to feel that they're participating more in the baking process, so they run to the store for fresh eggs to separate and bake white cakes. A waste. Buy Baker's All-White Mix. Tess reasoned. Who are *they*? They say. They will get you. They are rednecks. The *they* must be *us*, in some way, she thought.

Tess switched off the television. Her mind was becoming clogged by nonsense. She decided to eat lunch. She got a frozen dinner from the freezer, but it thawed before she had a chance to cook it. She let herself get caught up in the baking instructions concerning the exposure of all compartments except the corn. Why was the corn to be covered? It all seemed deceptive, covert. They said they would destroy us from within, she thought. Why not start with corn. Secrets. Germ warfare. How ironic, to destroy us with food from our own freezers.

Tess knew she was getting worse as the day went on. She was being consumed by senseless data, and fragmented details, without hope of whole connections. *Blungedank* was advancing. The second phase would be depression and morbidity. She would try to ward it off, or at least soften the blow, by taking a shower and putting on something bright and cheery—her new red dress, or the lavender blouse she had bought. She would put on lipstick, lots of it, make her mouth strong and red like the one on the mask, one that could not be ignored. It was then that her mother phoned with bad news.

"Hello, Tess, honey. You had better sit down. I have some bad news for you. Your grandmother is worse. We're afraid that they're going to have to take her leg off. Maybe you had better drive up tomorrow."

"Oh, God, Mom, why now?"

"Because they can't give her any medication to destroy those blood clots. It has something to do with her heart."

"Why now, Mom?" Tess wanted to slam the phone down on the bad news.

"I told you, honey, there's nothing else they can do. We've tried to keep her foot rotating, and we've tried to move her toes, but it's just not working. She's just too weak to help us. Her foot is almost completely black and blue."

"Not now, Mom. I just can't take it right now."

"I know, dear. I'm upset, too. That leg has given her trouble constantly. I told you this would happen. It's hereditary. I know it is. Her mother had leg problems. I've had these awful varicose veins in the same leg, and now you with that big blue vein behind your left knee. Honey, I'm telling you we're going to have to be careful about leg problems the rest of our lives. Granny is going to have to lose hers."

"Mom, I have to go. I don't feel well."

"I'm sorry I got you so upset, sweetheart, but you had to know."

"I'm sorry, too. I'm going now. I'll drive up tomorrow. Kiss Granny for me."

Tess put down the receiver. She thought she heard her mother still talking, but she couldn't take anymore. The second phase was bad enough without help from her morbid mother and the constant calls carrying bad tidings. Just last month her mother had called about Uncle John. A shame, she had said, cancer of the prostate. Poor man. And only a few days later there was news about Aunt Amanda's stroke—how it had left her face sagging and an awful drool from her mouth. So sad. And last week a neighbor had been mutilated in a gory car wreck. He died, leaving a wife and three children all alone. Just terrible. Now there was Tess's grandmother. Tess was sure that her mother was circling, just waiting for Granny to die so she could move in for the smell of death and bad news.

Tess loved her mother but hated that part of her personality— that gruesome facet of her mother's makeup. Her mother had always done it, made Tess feel queasy inside and scared about life.

55   *B.K Smith*

She had even scared Tess when she was little, with stories about strange men kidnapping young girls or other equally sordid tales. Sometimes Tess had even been frightened of her own daddy. Tess's mother would leave her alone in the car with her father while she went shopping, and Tess would eventually become afraid. She would remember the stories of big men with hairy arms, who offered little girls candy, then snatched them away forever. Her mother had never said exactly what happened to the little girls, but Tess's own imagination had conjured up the worst nightmares. Tess would sit in the car with her father, watching his face for fangs, and his hand for candy, as she kept her hand on the door latch—just in case.

Tess shook her head, trying to clear away the memories and terrible thoughts of her mother, and her father, who was, in actuality, as gentle as a lamb. He'd never paid much attention to her, but was certainly always a good man. Tess tried to get control. She knew everything seemed worse in the second phase, that the depression would leave her reason to rubble and ruin before it was all over. All bad things were magnified ten times over. She put an album on the stereo, hoping music might lighten her mood. But Tess sat on the couch and sank deeper into the cushions and her depression. She brought her knees up to her chin and stared at her feet, imagining them black, then blue.

Tess didn't know what time it was when Coy came home. He found her listening to Led Zeppelin and staring at the framed nudes across the room. She was sure she'd been crying.

"Hi, babes, what're you listening to? Is that 'Stairway to Heaven?' I love that song." Coy plopped his books on the table and headed to the refrigerator for a beer. She decided not to answer. She did not like Coy's good mood, nor his off-key lyrics from the song. "'There's a lady who's sure all her good times are gone. . . .' Hey, Babes, what's wrong? You look like you've been crying." Coy placed his arm around her shoulders.

Tess still didn't answer. Coy was getting on her nerves. She didn't want his arm around her, nor his scratchy five-o'clock shadow scraping against her cheek. When he hugged her and pulled her chin up for a kiss, she jerked her face away. She wanted to finish out the gloomy phase without his help.

"Hey, where'd the mask come from?" Coy asked.

"From work."

"You bought that thing? It's creepy."

"It matches my mood," Tess said, as she made a face.

"Uh, oh. That time of the month again, huh? Maybe I should leave?" Coy said.

Tess thought that was a good idea. He should leave for good. They should split up. They weren't right for one another. She hated finding his socks wrapped in her panties in disgusting bundles on wash day. She hated his gargling noises in the morning and his snoring at night. She liked science fiction. He liked anything but. In fact, he always seemed to choose everything the opposite from her. He ignored her love of romance, adventure, and the supernatural. He called himself a no nonsense kind of guy, a meat and potatoes man, a lover of sports, news, and the physical reality of day-to-day existence. Nonsense. What was the use? Tess was lost in her thoughts when she felt Coy remove his arm and leave the couch for the kitchen again.

"Mother called. She said that they are going to have to cut off Granny's leg." Tess glared in Coy's direction.

"Cripes, Tess, why'd you have to tell me that? I was going to fix a sandwich."

"You're a comfort."

"Hey, I'm sorry, Babes," Coy said as he moved next to her again, "but it seems like your mother is always getting you uptight about some gory thing or another."

"Well, what did you expect? It's true. I had to know. She's my grandmother." Tess tasted tears at the corner of her mouth.

"Okay, I'm sorry, Tess. But why in hell do they have to take a leg off? That's awful."

"Because she had a blood clot in her foot, and they told her to wiggle her toes and her foot or they'd have to cut it off. And it's all black and blue." Tess was crying again. She hated the depression. She hated being weak. But most of all she hated the smell of sweat and beer as Coy smothered her face in his fat, football neck. She wanted to choke him and his placating kindness.

"It's okay, Babes. Just calm down. We'll have a quiet night, and then I'll go up there with you tomorrow. How about that?"

"Just leave me alone. I'll be fine. I want to be alone."

"Sure, but I'm here if you need me, you know?"

Coy gave up on efforts to cheer her. He drank beer and watched the final game of the World Series while she sat on the balcony, shivering in an early autumn chill. Tess decided she hated fall, all the gorgeous colors everybody raved about. To her it just meant that rigor mortis was setting in before a cold, dead winter.

Tess watched Coy's face in the television light. His features flickered. His jaws were distorted with huge hunks of sandwich, moving up and down inside a thin ball of skin. He was ugly, very ugly, Tess thought. Why had she ever picked him? He had awful habits and he was ugly. He bit his fingernails, and he always had cold, damp, smelly feet. Why on earth did all her friends think he was such a prize—just because he always bought her candy on Valentine's Day, helped her in and out of cars, sat with her in the hospital day and night when she'd had her appendix taken out—just because he had big muscles and a hairy chest. Why? All those things couldn't help her overcome the depression, the personal funk, blues blungedank despair she had gotten herself into.

Tess felt a familiar sensation. The ripple bubbling through her body was so faint she hardly felt it at first. Then she realized that the third stage was beginning—the most dangerous phase of the dank. She usually became sadistic, skulking around, playing mean tricks on anyone near her. Even as a young girl, she had hated this phase the worst. One night she would be sitting happily on her front porch, watching a bright, full moon make powder on the sandy road that ran by her house. And then the very next night, when the moon had lost its fullness, she would become the Hyde half of Mr. Jekyll. The tricks and pranks were usually juvenile, but mean. She called strangers on the phone and breathed nastily in their ears. She called drive-in restaurants and ordered twenty hamburgers to go and never picked them up. She called her mother's friends and whispered ugly words through a handkerchief, or gave her own best friend, Mary Ellen Howser, a glass of vinegar instead of the glass of water she'd asked for before bed. Tess chewed bubblegum and stuck it on the bottom of her father's shoes and left rotten eggs in his golf bag. She had done these things most of her life, and the tricks never stopped. They only became more devious and well-planned. Now Coy was her most frequent victim.

Once, in the third phase, she had stuck a pin in his rump in the middle of the night because he was snoring. On the first try, he hadn't awakened, only snorted and shifted some. The second time, she had jabbed full force past the tough outer layer of skin into the soft, sleeping muscles underneath. Coy had yelped, thrown back the covers, and jumped on top of his pillow, standing with outstretched arms, palms against the wall, and one foot on the other.

"Tess, get up. Hurry! There's a spider or something in the bed. Get up!" he had screamed.

Tess had eased the pin in the side of the mattress, had flipped on the light and had cautiously searched the covers for the varmint. And there stood her Coy, trembling against the wall—a picture of pain, fear, and "dangling manhood."

Another time, while he slept, Tess had snipped a patch of hair from the top of his head. For days he thought he might be balding. Tess stared off the balcony and remembered all the mean tricks she had played on so many people, and she couldn't control the urge to plan more.

"Hey, Tess, come on in and have a beer with me. You're going to catch cold or something out there. Come on. I'll get you a drink."

Tess watched Coy walk toward the kitchen again. She couldn't stop herself. She went into the living room, sat on the sofa, and sprinkled salt into his beer while he was gone. He came back all smiles and kisses, then took a sip of his beer. And another sip. He sloshed the liquid around in his jaws, screwed up his face, and gave Tess a questioning glance. She pretended not to notice.

Tess picked at Coy all night, about his nail biting, cold hands, and smelly socks. He finally huffed off to bed, leaving her to scheme and plan her bedtime attack.

Tess slipped quietly into bed an hour later, and placed a pan of steaming water on the floor beside her. She listened patiently to Coy's slow intake of air, the uneven rasps and broken whistling noises. He was sound asleep. On her back, Tess carefully eased her hand down beside the bed to test the water. It was right. She could just see Coy's face when she shook him awake to tell him that he had wet on them. How embarrassing for a big, strong football star. He'd think something awful was wrong with him.

She felt herself grinning freakishly, and she could actually feel the evil twinkle dancing in her eyes. She lifted the pan, tilted it between his thighs, and let the warm liquid ooze under him. She knew she had made an error the moment Coy screamed.

"No, you don't! Oh, no you don't." Tess watched the light come on. "I caught you this time. I'm not asleep. See, I'm wide awake, you loony bitch. You did it, didn't you—my hair, and a pin in my ass. I figured it out. See, I stayed awake." Tess could hear the hysteria as she gazed at him. "Well, I'm getting outa here." Coy was out of bed and into his pants. "You're crazy, you know that?" Shoes on. "Why'd you do it?" Shirt on. "You better get some help, girl. I've seen that look in your eyes all night. I knew it. It's the same old pattern. Sneaky things, salt in my beer. I just can't take

B.K Smith

it anymore." Tess was amused by his smug look of revelation. "Good-bye and good riddance, Tess." The door slammed behind Coy, and Tess listened as he tore into the night in his old car.

At four in the morning, Tess entered the fourth and final phase. She never knew what to expect in the final stage. Sometimes she ate ravenously—pudding, pickles, bread, canned potatoes, almost anything. It was like having the "munchies" without the nice high from the pot. Other times, she made instant coffee over and over to see how many different shades of brown she could create with the cream. Tess went to her bottom dresser drawer and took out a tissue holding snippets of Coy's black curly hair she'd taken from him weeks ago. She sat down cross-legged in the living room floor, lit a red candle, and rolled the locks around in her fingers as she slowly recited an incantation that would ensure the return of Coy and his passion for her.

She felt bad for a moment when she reached under the couch for the valuable jade Buddha from The Emporium display window. She wished she hadn't taken it, but it did make a splash in the papers. She rubbed his tummy and made a wish for Granny and herself. He seemed to smile back at her. She vowed to return him to his rightful place and apologize for urges beyond her control. She would try harder.

Later, Tess just stared at the carpet, pretending there were little tribal villages in there if she looked deep enough or long enough. Her legs ached. Her back ached. She imagined the sickness slowly receding, downward through vein sap, around bone links. Gone. Nothing remained except a pink substance on her right, third toenail—maybe fragments of old nail polish, or just possibly the dank exit. She began to feel better.

Tess knew Coy was somewhere, shivering in his car, and biting his nails. Her poor baby. She would make it up to him. She wasn't worried. She knew he'd be back. Before the full moon.

INTO THE SHEMINAUN

for James Manasco, whose patient exploration
of the Phaistos Disk inspired this story

They were trying to ship him back. He just knew it. He had caught Berta on the phone talking to the doctor again. Another six months in that place and he would belong there. He wished they would leave him alone and let him do his work. He knew it wouldn't take long. He was so close to understanding the language of the ancient Cretans.

Treber Deacon scratched his rusty beard and flicked small, dry flecks of blue paint onto his work table. He pushed the specks around on the paint-spattered wood to form designs. He arranged them in sets of four, three, seven, and twelve.

It was all mixed up, but he knew it was there. He had to keep looking for it. He needed time, and couldn't think clearly with all the people around. He had decided that the museum in Crete would take his work when it was finished, if he chose to give it to them. That would keep his family quiet. Berta and the boys would finally see the importance. But he couldn't just think the work. He had to stay busy, not waste time.

Treber pushed back his chair, stretched his tall, thin body and moved around the room. The studio was his workroom, gorged with Indian relics, pottery, arrowheads, skins, and wall diagrams of Minoan and Nascan figures. He stared at a large rattler's skin stretched vertically on the wall, and thought how dead and empty it seemed. He imagined it coiled, ready to pump its fangs of poison and life. He counted the designs and thought how even God didn't botch this one—perfect diamond patterns of four, eight, then twelve. He explored the snakeskin with his fingers, avoiding the seventh scale. He remembered the old Cherokee legend of the giant devil snake—a man who looks beneath the seventh scale is to die, to be dead. He would chance it someday.

Treber glanced out the large new window he had built into his studio. He had told Berta he needed more light for his painting. She had agreed, he realized, only because she had hoped he would turn out more commercial nonsense for money. Treber really wanted a better view of Quaca Lake and the bottom edge of the Sheminaun Forest that loomed over the narrow lake inlet below. He stared from the window and watched a canoe slide across the smooth evening calm of the water. The canoe seemed small from a hundred yards up the hill, where Treber watched from his studio window. He liked the view of Quaca Lake from his home—a large wooden A-frame he had built mostly himself. He liked the way his home sat perched in the trees like an oversized treehouse. Treber saw the canoe disappear into a smaller inlet, swallowed by shadows from the dark Sheminaun.

He closed his eyes and imagined himself in the canoe, gliding across the water toward the deep green base of the forest. He wondered what it would be like to make it this time, to pack up all his work and just disappear. Hike into the Sheminaun and on up into the mountains where nobody could find him, or question him, until he had explored the ancient mysteries and could be satisfied with the answers. No talk. Only work and trees and quiet. Then he remembered the last time he had attempted to sever all ties with the modern world. He had lost himself in the forest for six days before the rangers, and his two sons, had taken him back home. Treber had tried leaving, but someone always stopped him. Someone always interrupted his dreams.

"Honey, you'd better go get washed up. The boys'll be here any minute for dinner." Treber's wife stuck her head into his studio, into his private thoughts. He flinched when Berta drummed her fingers on the door. He hated that. He grumbled an okay and pretended to go back to some last-minute work, hoping his wife would get the message and walk away. Instead, she came into his studio and inspected the room. Treber tried to ignore her, but he knew when she stopped behind him that she was glaring at the vacant easel next to his studio window. He didn't miss the small sigh of resignation, and he knew she was punching her chin with her thumb and forefinger as she always did when she was upset. He hadn't had a show in well over a year. He knew that she was thinking no show, no commercial jobs, no money.

Treber realized he was in trouble. He wanted to take her mind off his lack of business. He thought about starting a fight. A good one to clear the air like they used to have when they were first married. But he knew it probably wouldn't work. Everyone, especially Berta, patronized him now. No one wanted to upset the old man.

"So the *boys* are coming, huh?"

"Why do you say it like that?"

"Boys, sure. Twenty-seven and twenty-four. They're overgrown babies. They only come around every night so they can get a free meal. Can't cut the apron strings, and can't make it on their own."

"Don't be ridiculous—dear. They're your sons. They just like to visit you."

"Marcus is okay. At least he's an artist. But Stueben is a pain in the ass. Wonder which ready-made family he'll bring tonight. I wish he'd date a girl without kids already in tow."

"Oh, Treber, Lurinda's a sweet girl. And her little girls are precious. You love them."

"Ah, the latest—Lurinda—cute but too much a child herself to be a mother. Already, two kids. A regular built-in family for Stueben."

"She's twenty-three."

"And that little one, the one-year-old, what's her name— Linus?"

"No, silly. Her name is Linda. You know Stu just calls her that because she looks like Linus from the Peanuts cartoon. I think it's cute. And besides, you said yourself that you liked the kids."

"Only the four-year-old—Dawn. Four going on forty. She's more mature than Stueben."

"Why do you have it in for Stu today? Because he's still out of work? You know that ad agency has promised him a job."

"Some job. Nine to five at a drawing board sketching tubes of toothpaste or low-cal beer."

"Well at least *he'll* be working. I mean—he'll be able to get on his feet again."

Treber knew she was sorry the moment she said it. She put her hands on his shoulders and began to massage his neck and back. He clenched his teeth. He didn't want that. Why couldn't she fight with him. Why did she have to treat him like an invalid, or a child.

"Let's forget all this now, hon. You look tired. A hot shower will make you feel better. I hung a clean shirt in the bathroom for you. Come on now. Dinner's almost ready."

"Alright, already. Just give me a few minutes. I've got some things to finish up." Treber couldn't let her know she was getting to him again. He had to remember to get that lock fixed. "You know, nobody knocks around here."

"Okay, sweets. Sorry I bothered you. Just hurry." Berta puckered her small lips and kissed him on the cheek before she left the room.

"Money, hell," Treber muttered as she closed the door. "There are more important things than money." Treber switched on the light at his work table, then slipped a large drawing out of a box underneath. He reached for a pencil and began sketching small designs on his reproduction of the Phaistos Disk. He hummed as he operated on the penciled chart of the ancient Cretan disk and whispered a few words as he shifted the paper around.

"Logographics. That's the key. Don't try to translate, just feel it. You can't let phonetics screw it up. Just follow the spirit. The eye carries you, the sound, the instinct—to a simple funeral chant. That's what the patterns say. The logos aren't so complex if you're patient. Patterns of threes—repetition: Hear it. Numbers matter. All their talk about Linear A, Linear B, who gives a flyin' crap. This is more than just language. It's life and it's death. Right, that's it, just feel it."

Treber scribbled a few words next to the disk:

> *So it is,*
> *in death shall the spirits separate*
> *and pass into the earth*
> *and the spirit of man shall descend*
> *the spiral steps to heaven . . .*

Treber worked, deciphering the ancient logos. He tried to avoid mere translation, and he allowed his instincts to merge with the markings on the disk. At first, he didn't notice the door opening, nor did he see Lurinda's four-year-old standing beside his table. He didn't see her until he started to tap his pencil on the wood and realized the tapping didn't stop when he did. He turned to see the little blonde-haired, green-eyed beauty staring up at him from the table's edge. He scratched his head. She scratched her head. He shrugged. She shrugged. He stuck a pencil in his nose. She did the same. Treber laughed. He liked the patterns, and the little girl who seemed to catch every movement. He observed the large, dark pupils surrounded by the deep green of her eyes, and with his finger, he gently tapped the three perfect freckles across her nose.

"Oh, Dawn, there you are. God, I'm sorry, Treber. Did she bother you, or break anything?" Lurinda stepped into the doorway, carrying her younger daughter, Linus, who kept tracing a finger through the chocolate on her face and sticking it in her ear. Treber watched Lurinda try to push long, brown bangs out of her own eyes while trying to pull the baby's hand away from its ear.

"No, I was just finishing up. I've got to shower for dinner anyway. This kid's okay." He patted Dawn on the head and glowered when Linus screwed up her candy-covered nose at him.

Lurinda left. Treber hid his sketches under the work table and headed for the bathroom.

He shed his clothes and stood naked in front of a full-length mirror inside the door. He lowered himself for four knee bends, then stepped closer to the glass. He ran his fingers across his nose, and counted twelve freckles. He smoothed his beard and stretched his jaws.

"You need more sun, Treber old boy. Got to get out more, swim, keep in shape. Can't let them think you look unhealthy. You've got to keep Berta happier, too. Stop edging out of bed every time she touches you at night. It's not her fault. Her body's good. You just can't concentrate. Got to be smart, got to do it."

Treber stepped into the shower, turned the water on hard and cold. He ran the soap through the coarse hair on his chest and along his arms. He watched the lather bubble, then burst in the tangled light fuzz on his forearms. With his eyes closed, he began to think numbers. Four and back to three, six in life, seven in death to new birth. He formed images in his mind, giant sea turtles moving right then left to carry him into the spiritual underworld. He opened his eyes, then moved his fingers along the diamond-shaped tile on the wall and counted. He thought about technology—so haphazard, nothing fit, no faultless instinctual patterns to guide man. He concentrated on the patterns of four in the tile, then circled the drain with his big toe. He imagined twelve perfect circles.

Treber jerked his toe away when he heard the bathroom door swing open. "Hey, Treb, you in there? I gotta take a leak. Sorry. Had a few beers on the way. Lurinda's got Linus in the other bathroom. She got into some chocolate. You in there?"

"Yeah, yeah, go ahead. I'm not through yet."

Treber stood under the blast of water, letting it hit him hard on his face. He clenched his fists and tried not to hear his son talk. "Stueben," he thought, "rude ass. Poor excuse for a son. Why do they think he looks like me? He's such a strange boy, especially since he was fourteen, when he swung out over the lake on that steel bar and rope. Dumb. Let it hit him in the eye and nearly kill him. His eye hung there like a soft-boiled egg. His bad eye makes his face uneven, distorted—a bulging knot that puffs out his cheek. An ugly boy actually. He doesn't look at all like me. Nobody ever knocks."

"What, Treb? You ought to see that van. Marc and me fixed it up real nice. He painted the sides. Wait'll you see the fine, female bodies he planted on the doors. We might get arrested for traveling porno. The sound system's great, too. It'll blow you outa there."

"Can't hear you, Stu. What'd you say?" Treber hoped his son would give up. Then he heard Stueben flush the toilet and leave.

Treber eased out of the shower and dried himself. He slipped into his jeans and the shirt Berta had left for him. When he put his feet into his faded, blue thongs, he almost tripped on a dark object behind him.

"George, my man. What're you doing in here? Aren't you a little out of your territory?"

Treber looked down at a dark, green shell, marked by four perfect yellow diamonds at different points across the top. It was George, his family's live-in turtle. Treber wondered why George had strayed so far from his usual residence behind the kitchen stove. He knew the turtle only came out to nibble bits of food the family left for him on a paper plate near his hideaway.

"You know, George, you're the only one with class around here. You know what it's all about, just like all your ancestors. These other creatures Berta collects are pains in the ass. All these cats, dogs, and owls that gorge their stomachs with packaged seeds and meat. Cost me an arm and a leg, and they have no class. Yep, George, I could do without the rest of these hairy animals and birds around here. But, you, my man, have character."

Treber ran a brush through his hair, then reached down for his friend. He touched the ridges along the turtle's shell and probed the diamond patches. Treber counted, "Four, times three, twelve, perfection, order." He lifted the turtle and watched the lazy eyes unfold and the head disappear into its hard, green case. He put his eye close to the opening and tried to look deep into the black, hollow hiding place. He wondered what it was like in there.

"Come on, friend. I'll give you a lift back where you belong." Treber carried George to the kitchen, grabbed two chunks of tomato and dropped them in the paper plate next to the stove. He knew tomatoes were a favorite, second only to redworms. Treber gave George a pat on the shell and headed for the sun deck where his family waited for dinner.

Treber stopped and hid behind the den drapes when he heard his name mentioned through the partially opened glass doors. He observed his family through a small slit in the curtains. Flaubert, Berta's owl, was perched on a limb above the deck. He slowly twisted his head and rolled his eyes in Treber's direction. Treber knew Flaubert was the only one to spot his scowl. He hated the deficient bird with its broken left wing and tattered tail feathers. He wished Flaubert could fly away.

"Oh, Ma, don't be so hard on him. I don't understand all that stuff, but maybe he does," Marcus said as he reached for a large bowl of baked beans.

Treber frowned behind the drapes but thought how he could forgive Marcus. The boy was usually on his side. Marcus was strong and handsome. He had the perfect, high Cherokee cheek bones and dark brown eyes as sensitive and aware as a young buck's.

"It's just that it's all started again. He hasn't been sleeping. He gets out of bed at all hours and shuffles around in that junk room he calls a studio. He's been having those strange dreams again. I just know it. He's so fitful at night. And he's been drawing those things again—turtles moving to the right, then left, and those big birds with half-eaten rabbits in their mouths. He draws them on everything."

"Old man's flippin' again," Stueben added as he tore into a chicken leg. "I told you he was nuts when he went to Sea City with us last month. He spent all day watching the divers ride those big turtles in the tank."

Berta ignored Stueben's remark. "There's no money coming in. Our savings are almost gone. The only work he's done is a sign he painted for Dr. Harrison's vet hospital. And that was just a swap for having the calico spayed."

"Give him some time, Ma. He's got to get his feet back on the ground," Marcus said.

"He's been home five months for God's sake. Do you think I want to send him back to that place? It's just not working."

"Timber Hills is not that bad, Ma. I think it did Dad some good. He just got all uptight on that research thing he was working on, that old carving he was trying to translate. I tried to read up on logos and time crosses and Indian tradition. I didn't understand it all, but I did read that some people really get caught up in something called 'time locking' and logographics, and they have a hard time concentrating on anything else. They can't eat or sleep until they've worked out the puzzles. I just think Dad was caught up in that and he needs a good rest from it. Timber Hills was real nice. You don't have to be ashamed of it." Marcus patted his mother's shoulder and brushed small strands of hair from her face.

"Sounds like a damned cemetery to me," Stueben snorted. "T-I-M-B-E-R," Stueben cupped his hands and yelled out over the lake. "The nuttier they get, the sooner they fall."

Treber shifted his feet and felt an urge to push Stueben off the deck. He held himself back and thought, "I've got to get out of here. I knew this would happen—all their secret little meetings to decide what to do with me. I've got to calm down, control myself right now. Tonight I'll do it." Treber glanced at the lake and up the other side to the thick darkness of the Sheminaun.

"Shut up, Stu. Dad might be out of the shower," Marcus said.

Treber straightened himself and slid back the door to the sun deck. "Hey, what's all the fuss out here? Did I miss something?" He rubbed his hands together. "Man, I'm starved. This sure looks good."

Lurinda threw Stueben a forbidding look. He sneered and tossed a chicken bone over the railing and said, "Dig in, Treb. We started without you. Thought you'd gone down the drain."

Treber winced at the remark and wanted to slap the pitying look off Berta's face. He checked his anger, remembering he couldn't lose control. He forced himself to eat the thick, heavy food that was overcooked and tasteless. He tried to carry on normal conversation. He even joked and played with Lurinda's girls, and threw a piece of lettuce to Flaubert, who continued to eye him solemnly.

"Hey, Treb, done any weird paintings lately? Like dead rabbits hanging out of the mouths of big hawks with bulging eyes?" Stueben asked.

Treber jerked his head in Stueben's direction. He couldn't answer. He could only stare in disgust at the boy's bulging right eye that seemed to have no center, no form. It was colorless and unmoving.

"Stu's just joking, Dad," Marcus said. "Mom mentioned some of your drawings. Like those big birds with the half-eaten rabbits in their mouths. Pretty intriguing. Tell us about it all, if you want to."

Treber tried to control his anger. He knew Marcus was sincere, and trying to get him off the hook. He decided to give his family logical, textbook definitions. He didn't want to reveal his secrets.

"It's pretty simple," Treber said. "I'm trying to capture some of the history of the old Arizona Pueblo cultures. The circle of the bird's eye represents the spirit just as the circle of the rabbit's eye.

The dot in the middle of the circle is man and the physical. The ring and the dot represent a mingling of physical and spiritual. The whole point is simple, actually. Just like with the old Cherokee legends. When man kills an animal, like a rabbit, it must be only for food. The rabbit's spirit lives in the man until the man dies and can take the rabbit's spirit with him. The bird is usually a symbol of the spirit that flies to another world. And there's a logical count in the tail feathers, representing numbers in life and death. The diamond shapes represent life." Treber realized he was no longer making sense. He saw the puzzled look on the faces of his family. How could he make them understand centuries of Indian history and tradition in a few words.

"Turtle shit," Stueben snorted.

"What," Treber said.

"All that turtle shit. What's that supposed to mean? Since you've made everything else so clear and simple. Four big clunkers moving right and four moving left, and who'll get there before you. Admit it, Treb, your art's a little flipped out."

"Numbers matter," Treber shouted. He knew he was losing control. He felt sweat beginning on his upper lip. Berta and the boys stared at him, Flaubert shifted on the tree limb, and Lurinda fussed with Linus' dirty hands. The only one who didn't make him feel like jumping off the deck was Dawn. She smiled and held up four fingers.

"I'm four," she said, and everyone laughed and relaxed a little. Treber knew he had to think fast.

"Numbers do matter. I've been studying many ancient Indian cultures. They are all different, but original math is a part of each one. All primitive people used the 'fingers in the sand' method to count. It's simple. Math before zeros. All they had were fingers. Four fingers in the sand. Four on each side made a square, time crosses, diagonal, and then around made a perfect circle from twelve points in the sand. The overlapping makes perfection. Simple. Everything in the numbers, in the count, even the count toward death. The overlapping makes perfection, not like counting today. Where do you think we got our four directions—east, west, south, north? And the four seasons and the four phases of the moon? Everything in fours."

Treber was losing them again. He couldn't make them understand. He was telling them too much. It was his discovery, but he had to talk logically and that meant giving up some things.

"It's the same with the Phaistos Disk. Only the logos matter.

Each in a set of three. Each say something. If you can feel the ancient language, it can carry you. There is no black and white. It's a pure language of instinct." Treber struggled through dinner, and afterwards, he heaved a sigh of relief when everyone left the table. He could let down his guard. He felt as though he'd been on trial. Treber wanted to make a careful exit to his studio. There was so much work to get to. He had to get away before they questioned him any more. They were closing in. Even Marcus seemed unsure of him.

Treber walked to his workroom, checking to make sure he wasn't followed. He felt weak as he lowered himself into his chair at the work table. He propped his elbows on the table and ran his fingers through his stiff, red hair. "They drain me," he thought, "and they'll swallow every ounce of energy I've got if I don't get out of here. I'll leave in the morning. Got to get busy."

Treber pushed back his chair and headed for the closet. He plunged into the paraphernalia. He dug around for an old backpack he'd used on camping trips. Again, he didn't hear the door to the studio open, and he didn't see Dawn peeping over his shoulder at first.

When he found the pack, he jerked around on his knees and came face to face with the same green eyes that had teased him before. He let her help him pack. He pulled down the wall diagrams, rolled them into narrow tubes and stuffed them in the pack. As he gathered art tools from his work table, he noticed that Dawn had crawled underneath. When he looked for her, he saw her trying desperately to fold his drawing of the Phaistos Disk. He sat with Dawn on the floor and helped her roll the paper into a suitable shape for the backpack. Treber worked frantically, careful not to leave anything of use behind. He stopped once to scan his mind for forgotten material and saw that Dawn was repeating each of his moves methodically. She was seated on the floor with the pack between her feet, carefully filling the canvas bundle with pencils, books, and charts. She stopped from time to time as if to ponder the situation, to think of what she may have forgotten.

Someone knocked at the studio door. "Treber, have you seen Dawn? Is she with you? Stu's ready to go."

Treber quickly dragged the pack into the closet and lifted Dawn to the window ledge. "Come in, Lurinda. She's in here. Come on in." Lurinda opened the door to see the two gazing out over the lake. "We were just watching some swimmers down at the lake. Dawn's been helping me clean up my studio. Come on, sweetheart. Your mom's ready to go."

Treber helped the little girl down and placed a kiss on her small forehead. "Thanks, little bit. You were a big help." He watched Lurinda pull her daughter toward the doorway. "You kids drive carefully. Come back to see us." Dawn looked over her shoulder. Treber winked at her and she tried to do the same.

In the morning, a thin mist hovered delicately, inches above the lake, and nestled around Treber's feet as he shifted a folded tent and a box of canned goods around in his canoe. He stepped onto the dock one last time to survey his belongings. He looked out over the lake and up. A full moon was slowly fading, melting, becoming one again with a clear morning sky. He noticed a rosy flush spreading just above the woodland to the east and knew it was time to leave.

Treber glanced up the hill at his house in the trees and thought of Berta. He remembered how warm she had felt when he'd slipped out of bed and left her sleeping. He looked at the other side of the lake, toward his dark destination—the Sheminaun. He smiled, knowing the forest could protect him and his work. He liked the idea of being inside the Sheminaun, hidden within the patterns of paths and solid trees.

Treber finished loading, then stepped gently into the canoe. "George, my man, almost forgot you." Treber reached to the dock for his friend and placed the turtle next to him on the narrow seat. Treber lifted his paddle and pushed away from the dock. He watched the water ripple lazily behind the canoe. He stroked each side evenly, counting, "One, two, three, four."

B.K Smith

JOHN SMITH

J.B. watched television, and during the commercials, he contemplated suicide. If things get too rough, he thought, you just check out. People do it all the time. You lose your job; then you take a bottle of little white pills. The car engine steams, chokes, and dies at a red light, so you walk to the nearest bridge and hurl yourself down into the murky wake of a passing barge. No more small worries, or big ones.

J.B. had felt the push many times. Sometimes when things didn't go right, or sometimes for no reason at all, he was tempted to smash his car into the front grill of an on-coming fourteen-wheeler—to hang there, mangled and broken like a shattered insect. The headlines would read: "Head-on Collision" or "No Clues in Smash-up." People would read about it, exclaim how awful and would eventually forget about it—as easily as the truck driver, hosing away blood and wings from his windshield and grill.

J.B. could never forget death. He questioned even the smallest self-destruction—rabbits, warm and throbbing with life, that darted to their deaths beneath the wheels of his car when he went for drives late at night—or small frogs and moths that leaped to eternity in his headlights.

He had to question death. It was his family's way of life, his heritage. His father had introduced him to death at an early age. J.B. had been only ten when his father buried the cold, steel blue nozzle of the .38 in his chest and had shot himself. J.B. had run behind the house to see his father lying on the frozen ground, eyes wide and staring, with tiny slivers of a quarter moon cut into each. J.B. remembered hearing a neighbor shout, "He's shot himself in the heart. Call an ambulance. Get this boy out of here." But J.B. would not leave. He had thrown himself across his father's chest to try and cover the bleeding hole. He had wanted to save his father, to hold in his heart, to keep it all from running out.

J.B. focused on the returning television program. He hated _Quincy_—Superman of the Morgue, Captain Coroner, and Toe-tagger of all the nameless John Does who did themselves in with drugs or high bridges. J.B. hated the program because he always imagined his father on the coroner's table, with Dr. Quincy probing the empty wound, looking for clues and bits and pieces of a shattered heart. He sometimes imagined himself cold and stiff beneath a sheet, or sliding in and out of the cool storage locker, as Dr. Quincy tried again and again to dig out the tumor inside his

B.K Smith

head—the one that swelled and pushed and pressured J.B. into thoughts of self-destruction.

But Quincy could never find it. No one would ever be able to tell J.B. why he drove to the Brooklyn Bridge almost every night. Why he stood against the railing and stared down into the dark water. And why he wanted to jump. No one could explain his urges when he walked out onto the tourist platforms surrounding the Empire State Building. He looked like everyone else. Like the others, he put his dime into the viewing machines; he focused on the Statue of Liberty and the boats in the bay; but unlike the others, he felt the need to break the iron barriers and fling himself toward the street below.

J.B. watched the credits after *Quincy*, the endless list of actors, writers, and producers. He wondered if any of the unknown names were attached to people who considered suicide, people like himself, who sometimes lay in bed teasing themselves with full bottles of sleeping pills, or who held their breaths for long minutes in hopes of exploding their lungs.

J.B. knew *Columbo* would be next, mastermind of the gumshoes. He had plotted the four phases of *Columbo*. First came the murder. Exquisite planning on the killer's part made the deed an art. There was always a good reason for doing away with the victim, and always a new and inviting way to commit murder. In the second phase, Columbo was on the scene, sniffing out the killer right away, avoiding those with perfect alibis, spotting the villain on first sight. In the third phase, he continually harassed the guilty party with questions, probing and pushing for reasons and clues. In phase four, he snared the killer in his own lies. By then he knew all the motives and answers. J.B. had studied the pattern. Columbo never lost. He made it look easy. The murder and the solutions were as predictable as an old western where the Indians never won and the horses got shot. But J.B. wondered if Columbo could solve his mystery. Could the brilliant detective tell him why his father had left him with no clues, no explanation, just pictures of death on a cold winter night, frozen forever in his memory.

J.B. switched off the television. He sat in the dark, watching the last of the light sink into the screen. He lifted the paring knife he had been using to slice pieces of apples and cleaned off the dried juice between his thumb and forefinger, careful not to cut himself before he was ready. He considered harikari. He could sit on the floor, fold his legs, and let his hands guide the knife in and upward. He pictured his intestines, streaming out like connected strips of apple peelings. This made him queasy. He wanted a better way. He thought of driving to the bridge again. Maybe he would jump this time—leap from the railing in a graceful swan dive, leaving his dying breath, in a will, to the night air. Something to remember him by. It would be so easy, as simple as a jump, or the click of a revolver.

His Uncle Morey had done it, before J.B. was even born. He had just tied the rope to a beam in his basement, had slipped the noose around his neck, and jumped from a chair. Easy. He had carefully bent his knees during the jump, so his feet would not stop his fall. He was very determined, and no one ever knew the reason. J.B. knew they never would. Uncle Morey was a small-town publisher for the *Carl County Chronicler* in Virginia. Some relatives said he had had a nagging wife and too many kids for comfort. Others said that his paper was failing. J.B. figured that his Uncle Morey had just punched out, without knowing why himself.

J.B.'s grandfather had done it. No one ever knew why. His paper was a boomer in a thriving coal mining town in West Virginia when he shot himself with the 12-gauge shotgun. Some people had screamed foul play, but the family had the facts. Maybe J.B.'s grandfather had foreseen the death of the coal towns, which occurred soon after his own. But J.B.'s grandmother had always said it was a disease, a curse upon the Smith family—some drive toward personal destruction.

And J.B. agreed. Maybe it was a curse that made his own father murder himself—seventeen years ago today, on a beautiful winter night, when all was right with the world, except John B. Smith, Sr. Maybe it was a curse that made him blast a hole in his chest right behind the house where his young son was sleeping.

J.B. could still remember the sound in the night, like a Fourth of July firecracker magnified a hundred times over. He could still see the neighbors dragging his mother away from the body, and he could still smell the blood and the vomit on his own pajamas. He had tried to stop the awful bleeding in his father's chest. He had stared into the still eyes that held nothing but pictures of a quarter moon. And he had held himself tight against the hole until someone pulled him away. He remembered the wet blood, merging with the small red boats and planes on his soft blue pajamas. And he remembered being sick, over and over.

J.B.'s father had left him nothing, not even a note explaining why he never wanted to see his son again. His father hadn't even

B.K Smith

taken him to a ballgame, or told him the facts of life, or shown him how a printing press worked, or explained how pressures could build up inside a man's head until he thought it would explode. He had left J.B. nothing except his blood, and the inherent urge to do the same.

J.B. had never wanted for money. His father, at least, had left that. But J.B. never wanted it. He wanted reasons why an important publisher with a good paper, and a beautiful wife and son, would destroy himself, his business, and his family along with him. J.B.'s mother had survived it somehow. She sold the paper, J.B. had decided, in hopes of lifting the family's curse once and for all. She was set financially, but she drank too much now. J.B. hated to go home to visit her, and the house that still held nothing but memories and unanswered questions.

J.B. had not survived his father's suicide. He still read the scrapbook of old newspaper clippings filled with sports and news stories, features, and editorials that his father had written during his career. J.B. still wanted to be the writer his father had been during his years as a newspaperman, and then publisher. J.B., too, wanted to make an ordinary old zoo keeper come alive on the page with descriptions and dialogue, or scoop another newspaper with a hot story about corruption in the mayor's office. He wanted to write strong editorials, endorsing the best political candidates.

But J.B. could never match up. He had been fired from three newspapers for one thing or another. As a young reporter, he had written the obituary of a man alive and well in his hometown. He had gotten names wrong and had misquoted officials. As a photographer for the *Norfolk Advertiser*, he had failed to load his camera during a major hotel fire disaster. And, at his last job, he was fired because they simply said he had no talent as a feature writer. He had been hired because of his name, and as a favor to friends of his father. But the name wasn't enough. He had to prove himself. He had moved to New York in hopes of making a name for himself, and he planned to try Washington—an active and prestigious news center. And if he failed, he would try again somewhere else. In another town. After all, he thought, newspapermen come and go. They move on. Or, he might just end it and carry on the family's tradition. If he couldn't get a job, he could simply say goodbye, and save the world the trouble. He wouldn't even have to give notice. He could just fire himself out of life.

J.B. turned on his television again, to watch the news. This made him sad. There was something depressing about the news.

It was not a good word for it, he thought. News should mean the beginning of something—not plane crashes and murders, and new-born babies left in plastic bags on hot pavements in airport parking lots. He couldn't figure any of it—the greedy onlookers, circling like vultures around the scene of a three-car crash, or the looters breaking shop windows and vandalizing everything in sight during a blackout. Maybe this was the reason he couldn't be a good newsman. He hated the news.

J.B. could feel the pressure mounting in his head, pushing at the walls like a fat tumor, swelling with every new moment. He wanted relief. He wanted answers to the depression, reasons for all the human misery, reasons for his father's suicide, and for his own lust for self-destruction.

J.B. wrapped his fingers tightly around a lamp on the table next to him. He considered hurling the lamp into the screen, and he imagined the newsman's face exploding and shattering into a thousand particles of light and glass. He wanted quiet. He wanted to stop it all—the morbid scenes and thoughts that filled his mind, the questions, and the pain inside his head that grew sharper with every breath. He focused a moment on the paring knife, lying on the table, gleaming in the T.V. light. He imagined shining railings on a lighted bridge, blocking his fall into the darkness. He saw his father's eyes, piercing his own with slivers of moonlight.

J.B. lay down on the couch, bringing his knees up to his chest and his hands to his temples. He would not die tonight. He wanted another day. Tomorrow he would drive home. He would drive himself to the cemetery where his father was buried.

He would stop his car and sit for a moment, breathing deeply and watching an early morning mist rise slowly above the tombstones. He would get out of the car and listen to birds bickering about the uninvited visitor. He would remove a shovel from the trunk of his car and walk into the maze of headstones and plastic flowers. His steps would carry him in one direction, across the quiet plain of wet grass to one grave, to one headstone that read: *John B. Smith, Sr. May he rest.*

He would kneel above the grave, lean on the wooden shovel handle, and would whisper, "I want to know. I don't want to die." He would clasp the wood tightly with both hands, gaining strength as he stood above his father's grave. He would lift his eyes to the sun, just tipping the horizon, and then plunge the shovel into the center of the grave and dig. He would blow sweat from his top lip as he pounded into the earth harder and harder. He would dig,

B.K Smith

watching the sun shining on the shovel as he tossed each load of dirt away from the grave. He would lift the coffin's lid and would come face to face with his father's yellow bones. And he would ask why. He would probe the dark, empty sockets in his father's skull, looking for some light, some answer to all the pain.

And if there were no answers there, he would drive to his father's paper. He would break through the front doors, shattering glass and metal across the building. He would heave all the old, musty bound volumes of news into the floor and begin his search. He would shred all the old yellow pages as he read, discarding any page that did not provide a clue.

J.B. tossed and turned on the couch, rocking his head back and forth between his hands. He saw his home. He imagined himself bursting through the front door, confronting his mother, forcing his way into her drunken stupor, and questioning her again and again. Had she caused it? Why had she not washed away all the blood and pain? Why had she not tried to stop the bleeding from his father's heart, and the fear from his own?

J.B. heard familiar sounds coming from the television. He listened to the music from *Bonanza* and opened his eyes to see Ben Cartwright and his three sons riding high and free on the Ponderosa. The pressure in his head lessened some, and he stretched his stiff legs out on the sofa. J.B. remembered watching the program with his father years ago. He remembered Saturday nights when he would settle on the couch and wriggle underneath his father's arm, feeling safe and secure in his warm pajamas and in the strength of his father's body next to him. It was a peaceful time— with J.B. as Little Joe and his father as Ben Cartwright, riding their horses and together defeating all the outlaws and outsiders—with his father stroking his head and telling him that all the gunshots and blood were not real.

J.B. watched the screen. He watched the map of the Ponderosa burn itself up from the outside borders, as it always did before the show began. He felt love and hate for his father, a hurt around the edges of his moment of peace. He wished he could be strong. He wished that his father could tell him that he did not have to die.

RISING TO THE BOTTOM

There's this boy who followed me around the college library for weeks. It was several nights before I ever even saw his face. He would just slide his chair in behind mine while I was working at one of the secluded wooden carrels along the wall, and begin his "dirty business." Before him, the carrels on third floor were peaceful places to read, or to write out plans and proposals for my own library at F.Y. Holsam Elementary.

The first night he bothered me, I was just relaxing, reading *Up the Down Staircase* for the second time. I was leaning over my book with my head in my hands, resting my elbows on the only two areas of clean white surface left on the table top, when I felt someone bump my seat with the chair directly behind me at the next carrel. I was wary at first, wondering which species of library kook had decided to be my neighbor for the night. I knew the place was swarming with seedy characters, so I made it a point to pull my chair in closer and not dare turn around to see.

Eventually, my worst suspicions were confirmed. Slowly, and very carefully, the stranger behind edged his chair up next to mine. He coughed and cleared his throat each time he made a move. I felt him advancing on me. I was sitting up straight by then, with the table cutting my ribs. Then I felt it, his hair against the back of my head. Ever so slightly he let his hair brush against my hair until, finally, he leaned his head back completely against mine. I closed my eyes and felt the tiny hairs on my neck stand erect. Unfamiliar sensations moved down my back, like hundreds of little fingers probing at my spine. Surely, I thought, he's not aware of what he's doing. I'll ignore him for a while. Then his elbows began to move, and then the shoulders. He slid one elbow back against my waist very gently, and the shoulder rotated slowly against mine—quite systematic. I don't know how long I sat there, in goose bumps and indignation, before I finally jerked my chair to the side, grabbed my book, and left. I was disgusted, but I knew it was par for the course in this library—creeps in every crack of the building.

For weeks he found me—no matter where I went—to the second floor, first floor, back up, back down. Every time I sat down, there he was, nudging me, touching me. Nowhere safe. Finally one night I decided to face up to him and stand my ground. I was going to make him ashamed of his tricks. I slid my chair away from the light embrace of his sleazy hand on my hip (I can't believe it had gone that far), stood up, and looked at him—square—right in the eyes. He was not what I expected at all—just a skinny blond kid, no more than eighteen, grinning back at me with yellow, uneven teeth and bulging wide eyes. I frowned and walked away, deciding to report him and then deciding against it. Who in this place would listen? They're all alike. One big union of perverts—from the head librarian who looks like Chaucer's Pardoner, to the desk clerks who stare at you with filmy, red-rimmed eyes that seem to know what's going on but don't care. And, besides, what did I care. I knew I could handle the guy.

I saw him a few nights later, gliding sneakily in behind another victim, who apparently didn't care, because she let him move in much faster than he ever tried with me. Good riddance. So, I don't have to worry about his type anymore. He's drawing fresh blood. But I'm always on the lookout in here. It's a regular Sodom and Gomorrah.

There's this old man who looks to be about a hundred. He scuffs along the library floors, tapping his old wooden cane on the carpet with every step. He never stops unless it's to stand behind some young little freshman tease who whips into the library and only lights momentarily at the checkout to sign for a stack of books for a term paper. Sometimes he stops right beside me, and I can smell tobacco and moth balls in his tweed jacket. Maybe he's some ex-professor who just won't give up, who thinks if he keeps moving through the shelves, that somewhere in the stacks of knowledge there'll be a book to bring back his youth. I look at his old hand, a landscape of thick green veins and crusty yellow parchment, wrapped around the knob of his cane, and sometimes I feel sorry for him.

But, I'm probably being an idiot. I'm sure he's sick like the rest of them. It's likely he only comes to the college library to ogle the young girls he's seen outside. I have observed him walking across the campus, tapping his cane on the walks, and stopping only when some tanned co-ed jogs by or almost runs him down with a bicycle. I'm sure he'd like to capture one and take her home for fondling. He's probably as dirty as the rest.

This place is a little city of sin, a living breathing fungus of perversion and crime. It's a meeting place for what I assume are homosexuals. No longer do they haunt bus stations and bars, but they find cohorts right here in the local educational facility. And just take a walk between any book stack on any given night, and there you'll find a boy with his hand inside some young girl's blouse, and his tongue inside her mouth—oblivious to the fact that people might be watching his quiet little sins. Or, you might see one lone boy flipping the pages of a large volume of nude art, and flipping himself underneath.

There are thieves here who toss books out the third-floor windows to the ground below, and who watch their accomplices scurry away in the dark with expensive hard-bound volumes. There are destroyers of property—vandals who scrawl their hostilities across the walls. They scratch in names of people they hate, or etch in their own phone numbers in hopes other devils will join them in their evil leagues outside. Once, I read the words, "You are going to hell," scrawled across the desk top in one of the carrels. I couldn't resist. I answered back with my pen, "Then God only knows where you'll be." Later, I was ashamed and rubbed out the ink with my thumb. I had played right into their hands.

There are also the power-hungry, anti-establishment radicals, who scatter toilet paper, towels, and soap throughout the restrooms. Many times, after washing my own hands, have I thrown a crumpled towel toward the waste basket and missed, and thought what's the use of putting it in its proper place. But, more often than not, I reached down, picked up the paper, and carefully disposed of it. Just one small bit of trash that would've been totally obscure amid all of theirs. And I asked myself, *Why do they do it?* I suppose this gives them some distorted sense of power. It does them good to leave a toilet unflushed, to leave some deep, dark part of themselves floating around to prove they exist, and that they're here to disgust.

Then there are the quiet, timid, but stealthy types who plant their sticky gum under table tops, or throw it on the steps between floors when nobody's looking. They are the ones who splash cokes and drop crumbs into the carpet. And, I don't know how many times I've opened a book to find some strange substance lurking between the pages. These are the people responsible, I'm sure. I have catalogued them all. And all the little misdemeanors of this menacing microcosm are only reflections of a larger world of felonies and corruption outside.

I have to laugh when I think of why I started coming here. I thought it would be a nice retreat from my own noisy apartment building and from an obnoxious world. College towns are hell, and the rest of the planet has gone berserk. Students are up at all hours, playing tribal music, drinking, cursing, banging the walls and one another. Sometimes I lie on my couch, listening to pleasant strains of Bach or Stravinsky, only to have my lost world of harmony shattered by jungle beats from next door. Disgusted, I realize that my undisciplined foot is tapping the arm of the couch to the noise of something like, "I can't get no SAT IS FAC TION." And I know then that they are trying to brainwash me, slowly, in subtle subterfuge, by stages.

Other times, very late at night, when everything is totally quiet, I lie on my bed and listen to erratic moans in the bed next door. I assume these are supposed to be reverberations of some primal pleasure, conjured up to entice me. Most of the time I cover my ears with my pillow to smother the sounds, but other nights I blatantly defy them to corrupt me as I place a glass to the wall to show them I can listen, untouched and unmoved by it all.

There are so many disturbances and annoyances hidden in and behind the walls of my own domain—my own home—which is supposed to be my refuge. But it is not. There are televisions blaring, newscasters declaring doom with every depressing breath, little electrical shocks when the lights flicker in and out during storms, or when a big brown rat scuttles across my foot at the trashbin. And the rest of the world is multiplying like insects—millions of robbers, rapists, and murderers to watch out for, not to mention the dirt, trash, and clutter everywhere you look. Just too much noise and confusion. Sometimes I wish I could simply join my fish in their aquarium. I know it's quiet in there, deep inside the water, like a vacuum, away from all this turmoil. I'd like to drift inside their fluid realm, float down and in and out of those tiny blue castles and treasure chests full of multicolored stones. I like to press my nose against the glass, pucker my lips and move my mouth in a rhythmical contraction of opened and closed o's, along with the goldfish. We communicate. Or, I press one eye against the glass, to wink at the half eye of my blue, feathery angel fish who teases me from his watery world. But I can't join them. I can't even swim. There's no relief anywhere.

I thought at least in a college library I would find a different class of people—studious, upright adults who might seek knowledge and books, people who might want to share the common bond of learning and the solid atmosphere of scholarship. People who might want to make life better. I have to laugh. This place is no different. It's a tiny hive of bastardly business with its little rapes, robberies, thieveries, and perversions. I have dubbed it Peccadillo Library. It's as nasty and as noisy as the outside. I've tried other places, such as the public library. The librarians are always gossiping, buzzing, clucking. It's impossible to concentrate there. I've tried to find peace and quiet in the parks, but that's another story. Besides, I can't go there at night, and there are no books. I have to have books, even if they're covered with coffee stains and God knows what. They make the nights a little brighter, take away the shadows and disturbances, and provide order in a very unsettled world.

Day is not so bad. I'm up at six and at school by seven-thirty every morning. I keep my library there just as neat as my own bookshelves at home. I feel confident when students are assigned small papers on what they see and hear in my library. The reports have to be good. They see other children reading and studying— silently and conscientiously. No foolishness. I like it there, but the day goes much too fast, and then I have to face the noisy streets again, where passing cars splash into mud puddles, making sure they dirty my skirts. And I have to listen to clutters of people talking in shouts to one another, or stumble through garbage of some sort around every corner, and face a night at home with more noise and confusion. I hate to leave school, but even there I have begun to see signs. Sometimes I catch sixth graders holding hands under my tables, and not just once have I found clumps of pink bubblegum stuck tight underneath my chairs. I don't know how long it will be before I have to leave there, too. How long it will be before the outer corruption filters into that peaceful daytime space of my life.

So, I continue to come here, and again I have to laugh. This place is a jungle, a regular den of delinquency and debasement. Friday nights are the worst. That's when the lonelies come out. Black students shuffle aimlessly through the aisles between bookshelves, or along the stairways. I find them slouched or asleep on the couches like they have no place to go. And I watch the ambitious doctoral students, cramming the re-printed word and used ideas into their own papers, ignoring any original, creative words of their own. I watch them in their magic pants, squirming in their seats, almost to the point of denim-induced orgasms.

There are the piddlers, the ones who stare at a book without really reading it. They watch the words blur and smear into one huge ink blot while they fantasize and daydream. I call them piddlers because they waste the words on the page. They pretend to care about the knowledge while they're really thinking about silly weekend trips, or the night before when they rolled naked in beds of passion and lust for spouses or lovers. And, there are the

B.K Smith

usual frustrated rearrangers—the ones who like to misplace books to provide puzzling entertainment for those of us who must seem disappointed when the books rest among their ordered call numbers.

Then there's always the blond phantom on Friday night. He hits two or three girls a night—easing in behind them with the same routine—closer and closer—first with the hair, then the elbows, the shoulders, and then the revolting long fingers, probing and pushing. I do my best to avoid him.

It was on a Friday night that a student—a very stout, short, dark-skinned middle-easterner asked me for a date. I was sitting in the lounge, enjoying a cup of coffee, and engrossed in *A Farewell to Arms*, when the young man approached me.

"Excuse me," he said, "you seem very happy with your book. What is it?"

"*A Farewell to Arms*," I answered, then turned back to my reading.

"And the author?"

"Hemingway," I said politely, but a little annoyed.

"He's good?" he asked.

"Yes, he's good. He has a unique style. Very objective, very *terse*," I snapped.

"I want to begin reading American novelists. Maybe I will consider Hemingway."

"Fine," I said, "fine. Good choice." Obviously, he didn't get the message that I wanted to be left alone, so I closed my book and decided to ride it out until I finished my coffee and could leave.

"Would you like another cup of coffee?" he asked.

"No, I never have more than three cups a day. More than that makes me nervous." I took my glasses off and placed them on the table beside me and rubbed my eyes.

"Don't remove your glasses. You are quite attractive in them."

I didn't like the way he said that, but he seemed innocent enough for the moment. A foreign student—straight forward—probably used to saying exactly what he thought. He didn't know better, I conjectured. "I only wear them for reading. Sometimes I get a headache anyway," I said.

"That's a shame. Such a pretty head." He smiled a broad smile of even white teeth that seemed to light up his dark face.

"Thank you," I said, cautiously, as I started to get up.

"Oh, no, don't go. Stay for a few moments and tell me more about good books to read. My name is Hassan." He held out his hand. "And yours?"

"Lenora." I hesitated but took his hand. It was soft and very warm. I was wary, but he seemed harmless.

I talked with Hassan for awhile and told him several good novelists he might try reading. It was the first and most assuredly the last intelligent conversation I would ever have in this library, so I made the best of the situation. That is, until his intentions shifted. He actually asked me for a date—I who am forty and old enough to be his mother, asked out on a date, ridiculous. And I told him so.

"Age doesn't matter," he said. "We don't have to call it a date, as you Americans say. We will just have coffee sometime, when you are free, and *conversation?*"

"No. I'm afraid not. I'm a very busy woman, and I don't foresee any free time." I picked up my book and glasses, and got up from my chair. I wouldn't let him trap me.

"But here. Take my phone number if you change your mind." He scribbled his name and number on a piece of paper, smiled, and handed it to me.

"I won't," I said as I walked away, feeling his eyes on my back. I stuffed the piece of paper deep into my purse, thinking I would discard it later. I suppose I was a little flattered, but mostly I was disgusted that he thought I might be one of the gruesome group that meets here on weekends. "All the lonely people," I said to myself. "Where *do* they all come from?"

I'm almost afraid to say it, but I think I have found the perfect place here, away from all the perversions, the noise, the distractions. The basement mezzanine. A newspaper editor who visited the elementary school told me about it. He said he had done work here before, but that it was like a tomb and made him uneasy. I couldn't wait to try it. I asked the reference room clerk for a key and made my way down on a special elevator to the basement depths. It's fascinating. I have been here only three nights, but so far no one has disturbed me. I may never use the other floors again. The mezzanine is small and stuffy, but peaceful. It's full of old yellow newspapers, but they're stacked neatly and in order. And at least they are silent. They don't shout all their horrors and echo their disasters against the walls. I have started reading *War and Peace* again, and I am using Hasan's slip of paper as a bookmark, to remind me of what's going on above me, and that I want no part of it. Everything is so still and undisturbed.

The only thing that might pose a problem is the inhabitation

B.K Smith

of the mezzanine by cockroaches. I'm not sure how many there are, but I'll soon see to it that the library spreads sufficient poison to rid the place of them. At least they can't talk. They can't participate in loathsome human perversions, although I'm sure they have their own filthy ways of defecation and copulation. I have felt them watching me, observing my every move. Now and then one ventures furtively underneath my chair, or one perches himself, audaciously, on an old newspaper across the room. Others hide behind corners, and all I can see of them are small feelers, twitching as if to test changes in the air. At this point, they don't bother me, because they are very very quiet. And, I know I can eliminate them whenever I choose.

WITH A ROLL OF THE DICE

Eugene was comfortable in his worn brown recliner. He was settled into the soft indentions, with everything at his fingertips. His vodka and orange juice was on a T.V. tray to his left, along with the telephone and a spread sheet for the playoff games of the day. On his right was his tape deck and stacks of his favorite country songs. In front of him, six feet away, was the big color set he'd bought last year. He liked it that way—everything in order, everything within reach. He liked the idea that he could work and relax all at once, mix business and pleasure.

Eugene rolled his finger across the volume button on the remote control and watched the crowd at Three-Rivers Stadium grow silent. He liked to control the crowd from where he sat. He watched the people run onto the field, waving their arms and shouting in silence to their Steeler champions. He needed no sound to figure the thoughts of the dejected Miami fan when the T.V. camera focused hard and long on the face.

"Probably bet away his savings. Had to be a sucker if he put his money on Miami, even if they were up seven points. Nobody beats Pittsburgh in the playoffs." Eugene muttered to himself about the noon game, and smiled a little when he began to thumb through the book of names and bets on his lap.

"Looks like I'll come out about three thousand ahead on this one. Love ya Blue Dolphins. Lost it just right—by eight."

Eugene closed the book and took a sip of his drink. He picked up a cartridge with his right hand and slipped it into his tape deck. He listened to his favorite, George Jones, sing "He Stopped Loving Her Today" while he watched the last of the football fans push each other off the field. He laughed when the camera focused on the Goodyear blimp above the stadium. The vodka, his slow country music, and the day's easy win made him feel as light and high as the blimp hanging in mid-air over Pittsburgh.

Music from the upstairs apartment suddenly blasted into his drowsy world, mixing a heavy, alien beat with the mellow voice of George Jones. He turned up the volume on his tape deck but couldn't drown out the uneven thump of the bass from the stereo above him.

He thought of Niki upstairs and decided he might go up and strangle her. She'd been his friend for three years. Not by his choice. He had never talked to anyone in the apartment complex before. That was the best thing for a bookie. But when Niki moved in, all that changed. She was a young art student, too little to lug her huge canvases and boxes up the stairs to her apartment. He had to help her, but that was all he had planned. Niki had had different ideas about neighbors. She'd knocked on his door constantly, had him repair everything she broke, or anything that wouldn't work. She'd brought him her grandmother's famous chicken soup when he had the flu, and didn't care a flip, she'd said, that he made book on weekends.

She listened to his Korean war stories and his gambling tales, and had made him tell her over and over about his Las Vegas luck. That was her favorite—how he'd always won big in Las Vegas— about no-limit games, shows, girls, lights, and all the action on the strip. In return, she had reluctantly shared what she called her boring campus crud, but she could talk excitedly for hours about her art. He never knew what she was talking about, but he liked to hear her talk.

Today he wanted to strangle her. She knew he liked his Sundays quiet so he could answer the phone, but lately she had been forgetful. Since the new boyfriend, she'd forgotten a lot about their friendship—like dinner every Wednesday night. For three years, Wednesday night had been their night for pizza and beer or new dishes Niki wanted to try. With the new boyfriend came forgetfulness and missed dinners, and there was less order in Eugene's life.

Eugene decided to call Niki and tell her to cut off her damn stereo when the phone rang and jolted him momentarily from his comfortable position.

"Yeah? Well, Fred, you're cuttin' it pretty close. Frisco minus two. A nickel on Frisco. I got it. Game's at three, not four today. Tell 'em where you got it." Eugene placed the receiver back on its cradle. He wished everybody was like Fred, who paid every penny on time every time. Fred was one of the few dependable players. Eugene also wished everybody was like himself. When he lost the bet, he paid it. He was a dependable book. Men like him and Fred were few and far between. The phone startled him again.

"Yeah lo. A dime on Philly plus two. Yeah, got it. Yeah, Tuesday's good, about five o'clock. Tell 'em where you got it." Eugene hung up the phone and wrote $1,000 by the name of Carl Hansel in the book on his lap. He thought about Carl and his uppity wife. What would she think of her fine, upstanding businessman husband if she knew he was into his bookie for $10,000. Carl Hansel was all charm and good suits on the outside but a wreck on the inside. Eugene remembered the night he'd seen Carl and his wife in a restaurant downtown. Carl had introduced Eugene to her and had joked about losing $25 on a Cleveland game. His wife turned up her nose and hardly spoke while Carl squirmed to get away. Upper class. Eugene hated the type. He laughed when he thought of telling Mrs. Hansel the sum was $2500 instead. Carl was a loser, and Eugene let him keep playing only to watch him sweat every week.

Eugene slammed the book shut and threw it on the floor. He heard someone knocking on his door and lifted his stiff legs from the chair. He opened the door to Niki, and his decision to strangle her dwindled away. She looked too small and innocent, standing in the shadow of his six-four frame. And she looked too good in her tight jeans and blue turtleneck, the very same color of her eyes. He liked the way she braided her hair in one long, light brown strand, and the way she sometimes held it to her mouth when she was nervous or excited. She seemed to kiss it between her most important sentences for emphasis.

"Did you hear me, Gene?" she asked.

"No. yeah. What'd you say? Come on in." Eugene opened the door wider for Niki to come into the apartment. He loved the way she smelled when she walked by him, like soap, always like good clean soap and water.

"I said have you seen Bob?"

"Bob? Oh, Bobcat. No. Has he taken off again?"

"Oh, I don't know. I'm ripping mad. He scratched Rory and Rory threw him out. He said he hoped Bobcat took a U-haul to Alaska this time, and he wished nobody would find him."

Eugene was laughing as he listened to Niki's worries about her stray. She had found the cat about a year ago. He was hurt, and limping around the trash bin in the parking lot. He was a light gray with black blots, or half stripes, of fur on his back and face. He was wild, and his head was shaped just like a bobcat's. He had sharp ears and fierce eyes, so Niki had called him Bobcat, and then she nursed him back to health.

"You think he got into another moving van or something?" Eugene asked.

"I don't know. This is the third time he's run away. He's gone for good. I just know it this time. I've looked everywhere for him. He won't stay put."

Eugene remembered the last time the cat had left home. He'd gotten into a large moving van in the parking lot and had ridden

89   **B.K Smith**

with some family's furniture to South Carolina, six hours away. Niki's phone number was on the collar, and she'd gotten a call about him two days later. Eugene had made the trip with her to retrieve her Bobcat. The cat had ridden in Eugene's lap on the way home and had stared at him with hate in his wild eyes. He had slapped his tail hard and continually against Eugene's leg all the way back.

Eugene watched Niki pace back and forth with her hands on her hips. She looked so young, but determined not to panic. He secretly hoped he'd have to ride with her another twelve hours to pick up her runaway.

"Oh, maybe he's just flirtin' with some female friend over in the woods somewhere. I told you to get him fixed or he'd never stay at home," Eugene laughed.

"I couldn't do that. He wouldn't have any fun. How would you like it if somebody cut yours off? It's Bob's nature to move. I'll have to accept that."

"I wouldn't, I guess."

"I guess you're like Rory, huh? You hope I never find him. You hate him because he flushes your dumb toilet all the time. He can't help it if you've got a hair-trigger flusher. He likes to watch the water swirl around the bowl. Poor Bobcat."

"I'm not mad at the cat, Niki."

"His name's Bob."

"I'm not mad at Bob."

"Then what are you mad at? You've been acting really fuddy lately. A regular crab ball. You're mad because of the loud music today, aren't you?"

"Well, it is Sunday. I gotta work, and I gotta hear to work."

"Screw Sunday. You're mad all the time now, banging on the floor when Rory and me are dancing or playing the music too loud. What do you use anyhow? A broom or something? You used to be more fun. Don't you like Rory either?"

"He's okay."

"Okay. Just okay. At least that's better than what you said about Striker when I went out with him. You'd think you were jealous or something."

"That's silly."

"Huh! Well what then? Where is Striker anyway?"

"He's home in bed, sick, he says. He's a lazy college bum if you ask me. I'm gonna find somebody else to make book the next time he gives some lame excuse. I'm not paying him for nothing. He's probably doped up again or nursing another hangover."

"Look who's talking. I see you've been having a few today yourself."

"That's orange juice."

"Sure, and orange juice makes your eyes blood red and your gray hair grayer."

"You're pretty crabby yourself today. Is it your monthly or something? You look like you're about to cry."

"Well maybe I am. I've got something good to tell you. I think. And Bobcat's gone, and here you are boozing it up again when you promised to stay healthy. Nothing feels right and you're getting to be a real drag. So what if Striker likes to have a little fun. At least he goes out with other people, you know, human beings. He doesn't just sit at home and drink himself into a stupor. You used to be that way. What about the Vegas days, and the good old days in the cabin on Deer Pond when you used to be a slick gambling man?"

"God, you're on a roll. Why me Lord? What'd I do?"

"You're about dead, that's what. When are you going to start living again?"

"I'm living. I'm working."

"You're halfway. That's what you are. Halfway. This isn't any respectable nine to five job like you think. It's small-time book-making. And you're not on the other side either. You could be in Vegas again, rolling sevens like you used to do, and bringing home hundred thousand dollar stakes. But, no, here you sit, listening to Sammy Whinenette or somebody and drinking your gills full of poison."

"That's enough, Niki. Go back upstairs and pick on Rory."

"Yeah, well, I will. Go back upstairs. But I'll be back tomorrow night to talk."

"But that's Monday. What about Wednesday night? I'm making stew. My recipe."

"Screw your schedule. I'm coming tomorrow night after school. We've got to talk."

"What's the good thing you have to tell me? I could use it."

"I'll tell you *Monday* night, and you'd better be in a good mood. You'd better like it."

"I'll try."

"Can I bet on the playoff game today?"

"It's already started. It's, uh, twenty after three. Who's the bet for, you or Rory?"

B.K Smith

"It's for me. Rory doesn't bet. Well can I? I haven't exactly been watching the game."

"Who do you want?"

"San Francisco. Twenty-five dollars."

"Okay, you got it. I'll give 'em to you even. Can we be friends again?"

"Yeah, look, I'm sorry kind of. But I have to shake you up now and again or you'd rot."

"You're right. Okay. Well I'll see you tomorrow night I guess. Tell 'em where you got it."

Eugene opened the door for Niki and then watched her run up the stairs to her apartment. He felt like strangling her again, wondering where she got off calling him a crab ball and telling him how to live. But he felt like hugging her, too. She always did that to him—mixed him up and made him feel good and bad at the same time.

Eugene brought his bottle of vodka from the kitchen, fixed himself another drink, and adjusted his body in the soft folds and shape of his chair again. He pushed the off-button on his remote and watched the football game disappear. His mind drifted into the country melody of "Your Tender Years," and his eyes focused on the painting above his television.

Niki had painted the scene for him from a picture he'd given her of his cabin on Deer Pond. Only she had added snow on the roof and the trees and the ground all around the cabin. She'd said it made the small two-room cabin look more homey and snug out in the woods, just like a Christmas card. She'd given it to him for his big surprise on his fifty-first birthday last year, along with fifty smaller gifts—nail clips, cards, matches, calendars, pens, and small things she'd made or drawn.

Eugene loved the painting, and he loved remembering the seven years he'd lived in the cabin, after the army, before he married Marie. Sometimes when he sat and stared long enough, the water in the pond outside began to move, and he could hear sounds from the cabin surrounded by snow-covered trees.

He could hear all the big games again, chips clacking and scraping across the wooden table. He could hear Papa Joe and Red arguing over who was the best sweat player in the county. He thought about the women they had brought out to the cabin for luck, to give Casino Cabin a big-time atmosphere. He heard the women laughing as they mixed drinks for the boys and sat on their laps for luck. He heard the bad sounds, too, like the crack of young

Jody's shotgun when he lost two thousand dollars, drank a quart of Early Times, and blew a man-sized hole in one wall.

But Eugene always tried to hear the good sounds of his friends dealing and drinking, or the sounds of trees brushing the cabin. He listened for the frogs singing on the pond in the early morning hours when a game ended early and everything was quiet inside.

Eugene had met Marie when he was twenty-eight. He'd met her in a bar in Tucson when he was home for his father's funeral. He was low and she'd brought him out of it with her good looks and smiles. He guessed he was in love and wanted to marry her, so he did. She came back to Deer Pond with him, but wouldn't stay. He finally gave the cabin up to Papa Joe, and he and Marie moved into a small house in town.

At first she didn't mind the trips to Las Vegas, especially when he'd bring home $160,000 and slap it down on the coffee table for Marie to see. But she wanted the money in the bank or wanted to use it for a new home, or car, or clothes. And Eugene wanted it for his crap games and card games. It was his living and Marie had to understand, but she never did. He had to sneak out to Deer Pond for games, and when she'd had enough, Marie had called it quits. He'd spent all their money, and Marie wouldn't understand that he could get it all back, and more, with a roll of the dice. She had left him after two years, and he missed her. She had been good to him and for him. He wasn't sure he could live without her.

Eugene had begged her back, promising to give up his gambling and drinking, and he did for awhile. For two years he worked in a lumber mill, and he and Marie had a son, Paul. He loved Pauley and thought he was happy, but Eugene couldn't hold on. Papa Joe and Red had been trying to get him in a big game for two years, and he finally gave in. Eugene took the two thousand dollars he and Marie had saved to Deer Pond, and he'd lost it all. He came home drunk and asking Marie to forgive him. Then Marie was gone again, back to Tucson with his boy. Eugene checked into a motel and drank for thirty days, at least that's what Papa Joe and Red had told him after they cleaned him up and brought him back to the cabin.

Eugene sat in his recliner, staring at the painting of Casino Cabin and remembering all the good times and the bad. He thought about the day he left Deer Pond for good, and the days he had tried to get his wife and Pauley back again. Marie never came back, but he was still trying to prove to her he could play it straight and stay sober. When he could get enough from his bookmaking,

B.K Smith

he could get her a house again and show her he could be a good father and husband. He'd stop drinking and gambling for good.

Eugene stopped mixing his drinks and sat with the bottle of vodka in his hand. He closed his eyes to the painting and let his mind glide across the country sounds of George Jones, and he smiled at the mellow words of "I'm Not Ready Yet."

Eugene was disturbed by a knock at his door. He tried to shake himself awake, but his neck was too stiff to move. He knew he couldn't have slept too long because it was still light outside. As he lifted himself slowly from his chair, he noticed two vodka bottles lying empty at his feet. He cursed, knowing they had spilled all over the floor and he'd have to clean the spot later. He wondered where the other bottle had come from and kicked it under the coffee table. His left leg was asleep, and he tried to shake away the pinches and pricks, like tiny needles in his calf, on the way to the door. He opened the door to Niki.

"Yeah Lo. What're you doing back so soon? Did Frisco win?"

"What are you talking about? I've been trying to call you, and I've been banging on this door since four thirty. I told you I'd be here tonight."

"Tonight? But you just left. When'd you tell me that?"

"It's Monday, Gene. God, you've done it again. You just lost a whole day. Look at this mess. I see one, no two empty bottles, and that blasted country music is still playing. I heard it all night. I should've known what you were doing."

"Are you kidding? It's Monday? Man, I can't believe it. I haven't done this in years. I was just celebrating my winnings."

"Your winnings. Everybody bet San Francisco and they beat the Eagles big. So I doubt that you won the last game. You lost a bundle probably. What am I going to do with you? You promised."

"Oh, I remember. Did you find Bobcat?"

"No. I told you he's gone for good. But he'll be okay. He's a travelin' man, likes to keep moving. So you can take the tape off your flusher. He won't be ruining your toilet anymore. God, Gene, look at you. You look like death."

"I need to sit down a minute." Eugene flopped into his easy chair and watched Niki pick up the empty bottles and the T.V. tray sprawled on the floor. She balled up the spread sheet, threw it into the kitchen trash, and put the phone on the hook.

"What else have you done?"

"Where?" Eugene watched her move into the bedrooms and

the bathroom. He figured she was probably mixing up his toilet articles again. She hated the way he kept his colognes, deodorants, and after shave bottles all in one straight line on either side of the sink. Niki was always turning his life upside down. At Christmas she made him give up his artificial tree when she'd cut a real one and decorated it with lights and candy canes. She hated the plastic tree he put up every year. It was easier he thought. Put up the artificial tree and after Christmas, all he had to do was put the whole thing in a corner of the empty bedroom. No fuss. She always fussed. He liked his hair the way it had been for years. She was always cutting it in new styles. He liked Wednesday night dinners, and here she was on Monday, screwing up his life again. She walked back into the room, and Eugene smiled when he saw the pout on her face.

"You wanted to tell me something good. Remember?"

"Yeah, well, I'm not sure you're ready for it."

"I'm ready." Eugene watched Niki sit on the floor beside his chair, crossing her legs like she did when she was ready for what she called a serious pow wow. It made him nervous.

"Okay, tough guy. I'm moving to California with Rory. We're going to live together for awhile, maybe even get married."

"You're not going to finish school?"

"Sure, dummy. I'm changing schools. There's a great art department at Berkeley."

"You're not getting married? You're just going to live together?"

"For awhile. Just to see if we work out. So, what'd you think? Good news, right? Don't be old-fashioned, Gene."

"I'm not. You know I'm not. But how're you going to live, money and all. You need some?"

"No. Rory's family's got money. Besides I've got my big twenty-five dollar win from the Frisco game, right?"

"Yeah, right, you can buy lots of paint and stuff with that. Hey, I've got some good news to tell you, too, the real reason I was celebrating last night."

"What?"

"I'm going to Vegas again. I'm leaving this week. I'm gonna hit the Nugget and Caesar's on the strip and then plug 'em good in the no-limits at the Horseshoe."

"Sure. What about your Super Bowl bets coming up?"

"I'm leaving it. I'm gonna call Striker today and see if he wants to go with me. Let 'em find another book. They never pay off anyway. Not all they owe. The guys up top are gettin' fed up with it. I don't need trouble. I need to roll a few big ones and sit right for a change. I might even call Pauley and Marie if I hit big. Look, I'll show you. I'm taking my Vegas clothes to the cleaners today so they'll be ready by the middle of the week." Eugene went to the bedroom and brought out two silk shirts, black pants, and a jacket to show Niki.

"Yeah, Gene, that's really fine. Your lucky shirts. I love that black silk. That's Vegas all the way. You'll knock 'em dead again."

Eugene was excited, but a knot in his stomach kept tightening as he talked. He figured he needed food and a hot shower to relax him. He laid the clothes across the coffee table and headed for the kitchen. "Hey, you want something to drink, or I'll make that stew for us tonight. No, let's have steak and wine and celebrate."

"No, Gene, Rory's upstairs. We're going to start packing up. We're going to try to leave by Wednesday."

Eugene walked back from the kitchen. He felt a little dizzy and sick to his stomach, so he sat down again in his chair. "Well, that's probably good. I'm a little shaky from celebrating and all."

"Are you really going to Vegas?"

"Sure I am, and when I roll a few sevens, I might even come out to see you, okay? Eugene watched the skeptical look leave Niki's eyes, and in its place came the silver-blue twinkle he loved to see, like a tiny silver coin dancing from eye to eye. She reached up and kissed him on the cheek. The knot in his stomach eased and he almost felt good again.

"Great. I knew you would come around. That's the old Gene talking now. You'd better do it and come see me with wads of that green stuff."

"You'd better get outa here, so I can start packing, too. I've got to call Striker and get everything done. Maybe by Wednesday. Maybe we'll say goodbye to this town the same day."

"Great. I've got to see you before you take off. For luck. Don't forget. You better stay healthy, Gene. You've got to have good hands to roll sevens. You said winners can't drink."

"Right. A gambler is a loser if he drinks. I'm through with it." Eugene opened the door for Niki and closed it behind her as she left. He thought he'd read one last doubt in her eyes before she kissed her braid and started to say something else. She still didn't believe him, but he would show her.

He took his clothes to the bedroom and laid them out on the bed. He took socks and underwear from the drawers and neatly folded them next to his shirts and pants. He took two pairs of shoes and his lucky Vegas boots and placed them in a line next to the wall. He remembered how Niki had laughed at the spit shine on all of his shoes, especially his boots. She had kidded him about wasting his spit on shoes he never wore.

Eugene walked back to his recliner and straightened the tape cartridges that had fallen to the floor beside him. He took out the George Jones and slipped a new Kenny Rogers tape into the deck. The slow, country beat relaxed him as he leaned his head against the chair. He stared long and hard into the painting on the wall, and he watched the snow slowly melt from the cabin and seep into the freezing water of Deer Pond.

THERE'S A FISH IN MY SOUP

As I sit here on this plane, locked in tight beside my only love, all I can do is remember. I've searched the faces in airports, bus stops, campgrounds, motels, hotels, churches, and shelters for runaways. And I've searched the deep lines in Jesse's forehead, looking for answers to our life and our loss.

* * * *

Jesse and I give new meaning to the words "fire and water don't mix." We should've listened to that fortune teller at the state fair when we were teenagers, years before we married. The gypsy woman in her filmy paisley skirt and blue veined hands warned us that Jesse, the Sagittarian archer, was a fire sign who would someday pierce my heart and consume me with her passion. I, ever the dreamy Pisces always torn by two directions, was confident that my sign of water, male strong sea of power, would always cool her jets and douse her properly if she got out of hand.

Jesse's always been out of hand and just a step away from me. I think the fortune teller saw that coming, her eyes smiling and knowing as we walked out of the tent. I kept looking back over my shoulder to stare at the dark dot painted like a third eye in the middle of her forehead.

Jesse has always danced in and out of me. Even when we swayed to "Only You" at my senior prom and she gave me her sweet sixteen body on a blanket in the moonlight, I never felt that she was completely mine. Even when she was being defiant and rebellious, it wasn't for me, her black knight on the big Harley-Davidson, who swept her into the dangerous evening, her arms wrapped tightly around my waist, and her father scowling, arms akimbo, on the front porch. And the time I returned her to the porch at 3 a.m. because we'd lost all track of hours and fathers, she seemed to enjoy being grounded for a month, my Saint Joan of seventeen, who read eleven books while she endured all punishments.

It didn't bother her that the only one burning for our indiscretions was me. I missed her small strong body attached to mine on the Harley. I wanted to smell her clean washed hair soft against my face. Instead I raced by her house several times a night, gunning the bike in a loud declaration of my undying love for her. I knew she sat on her comfortable bed, that wide easy smile slowly drifting to the corners of her mouth.

99   *B.K Smith*

Jesse has always been in control of our passion and in control of our stormy relationship of 25 years. At nineteen, I did a two-year stint with the army and, reluctantly, did without Jesse. She starved me with her letters, which didn't come that often. They were always short but contained just enough to keep me begging for more—a subtle promise or a teasing of nights to come. I devoured her satisfying morsels greedily.

The day I came home for good Jesse didn't disappoint me. She whisked me away from the airport, and drove us to our favorite spot high on a hill in the woods near Deer River. I couldn't wait to have her. But, of course, I had to. She kissed me hard, then spread out a picnic, all while chattering away about how much she was learning her first year in college. The fried chicken stuck in my throat, and words about some guy named Nietzsche bounced off my ears. I thought I might explode with desire for this talking princess in green walking shorts and tennis shoes. As always, Jesse would let me go to the edge, as far as my control would allow, and then she would give herself to me.

She grinned at me, jumped up, and ran into the woods. When I followed her into the tree shadows and moss, she had taken off all her clothes. She stood strong and naked in the streaks of sunlight that danced through the birches, the ones Jesse had called her ghost trees. Her eyes were wild but as soft as a deer's. A part of me wanted her to stay there forever. "I always want to be free," she yelled as she ran through a stream and into tall grass on the other side. She let me catch her. She let me love her, and our daughter Terra was conceived. A wedding followed.

Jesse and I saw a play last year called *Glass Slippers*, written by one of her college friends named Brad. And one of the lines echoed in my mind as I watched the young female character snap a photo of herself. The line was about the camera's flash and how it seemed to be gone before it got there. I feel that way about Terra. She was four before I even realized I had this beautiful dark-haired daughter, whose stormy eyes and spirit seemed to duplicate her mother's. And Terra was gone from my life before I ever got to her, ever really appreciated her young wisdom and charm, ever noticed her wit or empathy, her dreams and fears. She was gone before I could reach her, drowning in confusion and disappointments. She ran away from us when she was fourteen. And for more than ten years we have been searching, trying to retrieve that "flash," her childhood, our daughter.

I don't blame Terra for leaving. Jesse and I struggled in our marriage from the beginning, from the day we decided like grown-ups to honor our passionate commitment or mistake, to provide a home for that precious life conceived on a land far far from the reality of married hiss.

And that we did—argue, fight—about finances, household duties, responsibilities. Oh we'd make up, come back, leave again, do battle, kiss, but the struggle—the push and pull—was constant. I don't suppose this hurt Terra much during the first few years of her life when Jesse was finishing school, working, making me go to college, and making me read books I didn't want to read. Or when she was forcing me into doing odd jobs, so I'd be a responsible adult and father, she'd say. All the while I knew Jesse resented me for the lost scholarship to study abroad, offered a few weeks after we were married. But she never threw it back at me even when I threatened to go to New Orleans to play my saxophone for a living or when I sank into a deep depression for two years.

And through the tumble and toss of it all—through braces, school plays, and skinned knees and egos—Jesse survived. Terra didn't. She couldn't see the strange bond between her parents, couldn't understand the dance of love and hate. She saw only the fights and the inconsistencies as she grew to a rebellious and stubborn fourteen. Then she was gone.

Again Jesse took over. I was lost through several years of forms, police departments, detectives, and futile searches for our daughter who was never found. I died; my hope died, but Jesse's never did. We had to go back to work, Jesse to her teaching, and I finally settled down in a fairly successful job in sales. But twice a year, for the past seven years, we have spent our vacation time looking for our daughter. Jesse follows every fragile lead and sees Terra everywhere we go. I am never embarrassed when she confronts and questions a young lady in her mid-twenties, just sad.

I think this trip to Arizona was our last search, no particular reason, just a feeling. We were really happy together for the first time. We actually did some sight seeing and made love under the stars of Flagstaff, and we laughed. I wish Terra could've seen us laugh more. I wish she could've known how much I love Jesse when she's bending over the frozen food counter choosing the perfect burritos or the way her skin glistens after a shower, or the way she kisses just my bottom lip. How could Terra have missed the way I feel.

We visited a strange little shop in Flagstaff yesterday called

The Not-So-General Store. We bought some unusual books, trinkets, and a can of Zodiac soup, guaranteed to float all of the appropriate signs. We both shook our heads no to the resident fortune teller. Later that evening we decided to camp on the store owner's land nearby. He assured us it was a sacred site, and we'd be safe there.

Jesse and I watched our last day in Arizona slip into a deep purple and crimson sunset at the campsite. And it seemed that all the bruises and hurts from the past ten years were fading with it. She smiled at me over her lantern when she settled in with one of her new books. I decided to cook the soup, brew a pot of coffee, and toast some bread for our dinner. That pleased her.

Jesse's real passion was always knowledge, movement, progression. I think I was an afterthought who couldn't keep up, but she kept me—out of some sense of devotion or duty or maybe out of love. I've never been sure, only thankful. Glad that the two years I was depressed and out of work she propped me up, worked two jobs, bought our home, loved our daughter, took care of us.

I took Jesse a steaming mug of soup and a cup of coffee. Then I snuggled in next to her arm as she dipped her spoon in and out of her mug.

"What's wrong?" I asked. "Don't you like it?"

"There's a fish in my soup," she laughed.

"Always has been," I said.

I loved seeing Jesse's smile again, not the white-lipped, tense line across her mouth from past years, but this smile, drifting slowly to the corners.

Abe, the store owner, seemed to come from out of nowhere. His voice startled Jesse and me. He was holding a lantern, and a rope with an old mule at the end of it. "Howdy folks. How'd ya like this spot? Told you it's a good one, didn't I?"

"It's great," I said.

"So pretty and quiet," Jesse added. "Would you like a cup of coffee?"

"Sure, don't mind if I do." Abe spit a clump of tobacco onto the ground behind the mule. "That wouldn't mix too good, would it?" Abe sat down on a large metal cooler to sip his hot coffee slowly.

"Where you headed?" I asked.

"Oh me and my friend here just came to check on you kids. I gotta put him in the barn for the night. I guess you saw it a ways down the road when you came in?"

"What's his name?" I asked.

"Well, this is old Habit. He's about fifteen years old, believe it or not."

"Habit?" Jesse giggled. "Why Habit?"

"Oh I had him about five years before I called him anything but mule. Then I decided we'd been together so long, got so used to one another, I'd call him Habit. You know what I mean. Don't have to talk. Just kinda know what the other one needs. Get used to it, and it makes you feel safe and satisfied."

"That's a great name," I said.

"That's a good name for you, Daniel," Jesse laughed.

"Thanks."

Abe didn't hang around long. He drank his coffee, wished us a safe trip home, and wandered off.

Jesse waited until he'd gone a distance when she said, "I believe Abe's smarter 'n he looks and sounds, don't you?"

"Yep, fifteen years? Fifteen? I guess old habits die hard, huh?" I laughed.

"Oh, gimme a break," Jesse said.

Jesse and I slept close last night, and I've never felt so much love for her than when I kissed her goodnight under those Flagstaff stars, on Abe's sacred site.

* * * *

And today Jesse thinks she's seen her again—an airline hostess in her mid-twenties—just getting off the plane as we got on.

"But the girl had blonde hair," I say quietly.

"She could've dyed it. She has Terra's eyes. Let me just . . . ."

I place my hand on Jesse's as the plane jerks forward. "No, you're tired," I say. "Let's go home."

B.K Smith

A CITY PASTORAL

The sun seeped through a city haze of factory smoke and smog on the rooftop of the Chicago tenement. Light sifted through thin clouds of damaged air to settle lightly on the flat, gray surface of the roof, on the dull green trash bin in the corner, and on the heads of Val and Marco, who dealt with the death of their friend silently and separately.

Val Martinez sat on the warm rooftop and leaned his head back against a large cardboard box. He closed his eyes to shade them from a glaring mid-July sun as he rolled a baseball back and forth between the fingers and thumb of his right hand. Val felt comfort from the box behind his head, from the huge target of red, white, and blue circles painted on one side of the worn refrigerator box stuffed with old newspapers and rags. He rested his head against a smaller black circle in the middle of the others—the bull's eye of Eddie's target box.

Val shifted the baseball in his hand as he imagined his friend preparing for a curve ball or his famous slider. He could see Eddie, a tall six feet of control, standing straight and proud on the mound, his black eyes fastening on the batter, and then the catcher's signals. He could see Eddie on the roof, winding for a hard pitch to the center of his target box, and Val remembered the ripping sound of the ball against the firmly packed cardboard—like a shot—high above the city. He wanted to hear it again.

A few feet away, Marco Manuel leaned slightly over the concrete wall, bordering the tenement's roof. He rested his elbows on the hard, hot grainy surface as he stared at the street twelve floors down. Marco imagined the broken body of his dead friend Eduardo Rodriguez lying on the empty sidewalk below. He could see Eddie's arm, smashed, and dangling limply over the curb. He stared harder until he saw the blood trickle down Eddie's arm, moving from shoulder to bicep, around the elbow, to the wrist, off the forefinger, down into the street drain, and out of sight. He shook his head to clear away the images. Eddie was dead, and that was that, Marco thought. He had jumped to forget his problems and had left his friends behind to remember. He had left Marco with the weight of truth on his shoulders, the reason he chose to die, and the choice to carry out the horrible duty of killing the memory of a king.

A cab pulled up to the curb below, and Marco strained his eyes again to recognize three women dressed in black who emerged from the yellow car. "There's Mrs. Rodriguez and Eddie's sister," Marco said. "I guess they've come from the church. Someone's with them. I can't tell who it is."

"It's Maria. She went with them to light candles for Eddie." Val lifted his T-shirt to wipe the sweat from his forehead, then shaded his face with his arm as he looked to Marco.

"Your sister is acting pretty big. She rode with the family to the grave side this morning, didn't she?" Marco asked.

"She's not so little anymore. Maybe just fifteen, but she acts like a woman now since Eddie is gone. She's learned about life and death too soon, Father Rico said. She's been with Mrs. Rodriguez every day, helping with the funeral and watching over the kids."

"Mrs. Rodriguez is going to the sidewalk where Eddie fell," Marco said.

"Maria says she won't leave it alone. She says Mrs. Rodriguez stands on the very place and cries for Eddie to come back."

"There goes Maria to pull her away. Should we go down to help?" Marco asked.

Val stood up and slowly walked to Marco's side. "No, she can handle it. She'll get Mrs. Rodriguez into the building. She'll tell her how she loved Eddie, too, and that they should mourn him together in his home. Maria explained it all to me." Val raised himself onto the concrete wall and sat on the edge.

"Jesus, man you'd better be careful. You could drop right over the edge like Eddie," Marco said.

"Don't be stupid. We've been on the rooftop all our lives. We've even walked this wall. Why are you chicken all of the sudden?"

"Eddie walked the wall, but he fell, didn't he Val?"

"How could he fall? He could walk this wall with his eyes closed. Better than anybody." Val eased himself down from the ledge and pretended to be concerned with his sister, who helped Mrs. Rodriguez into the building.

"So what do you think happened?" Marco asked.

Val could feel his friend's eyes on him. "I don't know." .

"Some people are saying that maybe Eddie took drugs," Marco said.

"Don't talk crazy. I know how Eddie felt about drugs. He hated that scene. He said his body was his temple. He was religious about it. He was in control of his body. Good foods, no alcohol, no drugs."

"Sure I know. That's just talk. Eddie was king, right? King

of the Hardball. I'll bet if we could've clocked his pitch last week, it would've been over eighty miles per hour. He could burn a glove, couldn't he?" Marco asked.

"Right. What an arm. He could knock you down." Val punched playfully at Marco's shoulder. They were glad to laugh. "I know I could've clocked his pitch at 120 up here on the roof that day in April when he was pitching practice at his target box against Juan Matilla. I was stuffing the box from inside with more paper and rags when he let one go at the target. I felt the thunder for a week. That ball shook the whole building when it hit."

"I remember that day," Marco said. "He was proving himself to Juan. He was 160 pounds of competition, that Eddie. He was hitting dead center and busting the box. We had to make a new target every time, didn't we?"

"Yeah, he made the great Juan Matilla look like little league," Val answered, and the boys laughed hard and loud.

"And remember that white boy Joey Pete Johnson who thought he'd take Eddie in tryouts? He thought he'd be pitching for the Panthers?" Marco asked.

"Yeah. Eddie threw strong that day. He pitched smooth and graceful like a cat," Val said.

"He pounded Joey Pete Johnson onto the bench," Marco said.

"And Joey threw a handful of dirt at Eddie when try-outs were over and called him a Chicano coffee bean. But Eddie didn't pay him any attention. He just winked and said that control is the key, and winning comes with control," Val said.

"What a pitch. He could knock over a building," Marco said. "No wonder those white boys were jealous. Joey was so mad he could've tossed Eddie off the roof."

Val frowned. He felt anger building inside him when he thought of someone pushing his friend from the rooftop. He was behind Eddie's eyes. Val imagined the green-eyed boy coming toward him. He could feel the boy's hand on his chest, pushing him over the edge and into the empty air. Val could see the boy's mouth spread open into a snarl of huge white teeth. He tried to scream, but the wind filled his cheeks and sucked all the sound away. He tried to close his eyes, but again the wind blew back the lids—holding them open so he would have to watch the blur of sky and skyscrapers. He tried to pump his arms and legs like wings, but only succeeded in rolling over, a tangled mass, facing the sidewalk that grew large and square as he fell.

"Val. What're you thinking, Val?" Marco shook his friend.

"Nobody pushed Eddie. Who could do that?" Val asked.

"No," Marco said, "I know that. Eddie pushed himself."

"What?"

"I mean he just lost his balance."

"Eddie never lost his balance. He was always in control. He was a winner. He was smooth and graceful and balanced."

"Well, it can happen," Marco said. "When I was learning to dive from the high board at the pool, it happened to me. It was about six years ago. I was only ten, just a kid. Anyway, I stood on the end of the board for a long time; then I went to my knees for a while. Then I just sat down and stared over the edge into the water. I stared so long and leaned so far over, it was like I was hypnotized. I lost control. I just fell off, just like that. The next thing I knew, I hit the water on my face."

"That wouldn't happen to Eddie," Val said.

"Even if he walked along the edge of this wall? Maybe he thought he could fly. What an arm. He probably could fly if he wanted to. With that arm."

"Shut up, Marco. That's not funny."

"I was serious." Marco wasn't serious. He wanted to take away the pain from Val's eyes. He wanted to take away the puzzles. But he didn't know how. He wanted to move slow and easy like Eddie would've done it. But everything he said came out a joke or a foolish notion about Eddie's fall. He wished he could cut out his tongue so the truth could lie silently in his mouth forever. "Come on, let's play some catch. The sun's going down some. It's cooler now," Marco said.

"Sure. I'll get the gloves and ball," Val said, happy to move away from the wall to the solid rooftop. He walked to a nearby corner to pick up their gloves. "You just watch what you say, friend."

Marco followed Val with his eyes. His friend, sixteen, the same as him but acting so much younger. His dark face, smooth like a child's, his eyes innocent as he tossed Eddie's ball into one of the gloves. Marco's throat hurt, as if he'd swallowed the ball and let it stick. There was no good way to tell Val that Eddie was no hero, that he was scared like everybody else. He didn't know how to say it. Things like that should be left to people who knew the words, like Father Rico. Marco could think it out. It sounded good inside. But everything outside was wrong. He was losing his nerve. He was falling like Eddie, grasping nothing, trying to hold onto air, flinging his arms and legs in every direction. He could see the sidewalk. He opened his mouth to scream, but the wind rushed into his lungs to explode them.

"Toss one like Eddie," Val said as he threw Marco a glove and the ball. He waited for the first pitch.

Marco threw easily.

"That's no pitch. Make it pop my glove, Marco."

"Start slow, Val. Let's warm up our arms." He caught Val's pitch and threw to him again. "You know, Val, maybe Eddie is better off now."

"What's that supposed to mean?"

"Well, maybe Eddie couldn't make it to the big leagues."

"That's crazy. He could've had it all." Val threw the ball harder.

"Some people are saying that maybe he wouldn't break into the majors, saying he was Chicano minority, and nobody was scouting him."

"You know that's bull. Chicanos can make it today. If they're good. The black brothers took over the roundball and football. But Chicanos are baseball. Eddie was good. He could've had anything—Cadillacs and houses. He could've bought us a whole team."

"What about last year, Val? What the coach said when Eddie threw his arm out. He said it might never be good again. He said Eddie might need operations, that his arm might never be strong enough for the majors."

"We saw him, Marco. You know he was the best. The king. I'll bet if we'd clocked his pitch last week, the ball would've been at 150. His arm was good." Val threw the ball as hard as he could.

"Hey, take it easy, man. You might hurt somebody." Marco lifted his arm to return the ball, and Val threw his own glove back into the corner.

"Forget it," Val said. "I'm tired of this anyway. You throw like a woman." He walked to the target box and plopped himself down against the cardboard.

"You know what we should do with Eddie's target box, Marco? We should bronze it. We should write on it *In Memory of Eduardo Rodriguez—King of the Hardball.* We can't let them throw this out. It's a monument."

"What about all the graffiti?" Marco laughed.

"We'll bronze that, too." Val ran his fingers along the battered edges.

"Hey, here's a good one. *Juanita is hot for Eddie,*" Marco read.

"He was really hot with the women, I tell you. Juanita sure pulled up her skirts for Eddie when he wanted it."

"You're wrong," Val said.

"What. Everybody knows Juanita spread her legs for Eddie. She wasn't just interested in his pitching arm like us, you know," Marco said.

"I know different," Val said.

"So what're you talking about? How can you act so smart about it?"

"Eddie was not with the ladies."

"Make sense."

"Eddie and me talked a lot, Marco. He never had women. He said he wanted to keep his body strong for baseball. He said women make you weak. Eddie resisted their temptations."

"They make you weak for sure. That Juanita made me weak here on the rooftop last month. You ever been weak, Val?"

"We talked, Marco. It's all true. Eddie said women were no good for his career. He was in control."

"You telling me Eduardo Rodriguez was a virgin? You telling me he died before he lived it up?"

"Don't make jokes, Marco."

"What an arm. He could knock you over but he could never knock you up, right Val?" Marco tried to laugh. He felt nervous and weak. Nothing was coming out right. His words felt rough and ugly as they tumbled from his lips. He wanted to laugh all the hurt away. And he wanted to cry.

"Shut up, Marco. I'll take you out, I swear."

"Come on, Val. Be wise. Look around you. What about Maria?"

"What about Maria?" Val asked.

"The rumors about Eddie and your little sister."

"What rumors? What are you saying? Quick, say it."

"That maybe why Eddie jumped was Maria. That maybe she is pregnant with Eddie's baby. Maybe he couldn't think of losing his career. Maybe lots of things," Marco said.

"I'll kill you, Marco." Val grabbed for Marco's throat and landed on top of him. He tried to hit Marco, but his friend was stronger. He pushed Val back into the target box until it burst beneath their fighting. They scrambled in the rags and paper, punching at one another, swinging blindly, and wrestling among torn cardboard until Marco flipped Val onto his back and placed his knees on Val's arms.

"It's true, Val. I swear it's true."

"Say you're sorry. Say you'll die before you ever say those words to anybody again. Say it."

"I can't, Val. Eddie talked to me, too. Maria is pregnant. She's carrying Eddie's baby. He couldn't take it, losing his arm, no money to take care of Maria."

"Jesus, Marco, that's my sister."

"I know. I'm sorry, but it's true. He told me, up here on the roof just a few nights ago. Right here. He stood on the wall. He said he would jump. He cried, Val."

"He wouldn't kill himself."

"He did, Val. I swear it. God, I didn't know he would really do it. I had to tell. I've been crazy with it."

"Let me up," Val said quietly. Tears of anger and pain mixed with the sweat and blood in the corner of his mouth. Marco released him, and Val stood in the scattered ruins of Eddie's monument. He kicked the torn pieces of cardboard. He lifted the remains of the target, walked to the concrete wall, and threw them over the side. Marco followed with other pieces of rags and paper. The boys worked silently, pitching the fragments into the air and watching them fall to the street until there was nothing left of the box. Val turned his back to the wall and slid down against the concrete. He brought his knees up to his chest, folded his arms, and lowered his head onto them.

"I'm sorry, Val. You had to know."

"Don't say anymore."

"Eddie was human. Like you and me."

"He was more."

"I know. He was king, King of the Hardball. We won't forget," Marco said as he looked to the street below. He watched the pieces of Eddie's target box, like clean white bones, lying on the sidewalk. He watched the wind pick them up and scatter them along the street. He knew he hadn't said the right things. He had handled it all wrong. But he felt relieved.

"I loved him," Val said.

"I know."

"We'll take care of Maria."

"Sure we will," Marco said. "And Father Rico will help."

"She'll have Eddie's baby," Val said as he stood up next to his friend and rested his arms on the wall. They looked out over the city, cleaner and quieter before twilight, after most of the factories and machines had stopped for the day.

"Sure, and he'll have a good arm. We'll see to that."

Val smiled and lifted his eyes to the sunset. He imagined Eddie winding, then tossing the sun across the length of the Chicago skyline. He clocked it at 200.

Session #22

"What we have here, Doc, is a manic-depressive in love with a schizophrenic." Peter gave me one of his slow, easy smiles, his full lips spreading over even white teeth, accentuated by dark olive skin and a five o'clock shadow he can never seem to shave away. I suppose if I were ever going to fall in love with one of my clients, it would have to be Peter, this talented young man of twenty-nine, who seems to carry the weight of the world in his sad blue eyes and in his art. I try to discourage gifts from patients, but his bas-relief of dancing ladies hangs above the couch where he has sat during our sessions for the past eleven months.

"No comment?" Peter asked.

"I was wondering what makes you still see yourself as a manic depressive."

"It was just a joke, Doc. I don't have too many really manic or happy days anymore. And the Prozac helps keep the deep dives away. So, I guess you guys are right. I'm *simply* suffering from depression."

"What would make you really happy?" I asked.

"I have no earthly idea."

"Would having Penelope make you happy?"

"As much as any addiction, I guess. Isn't that what you called her, an addiction? Don't you think she has a split personality? I mean, this has been going on for three years. One day I hear this sweet soft voice that promises me she'll leave her husband and be with me. The next day she won't talk to me and may not for three months."

"We've discussed that behavior. It's called approach/avoidance."

"What are you writing over there—that I'm nuts? Or are you just doodling, like I do when I'm sick to death of listening to somebody talk."

"I write down responses from you, exact quotes. I may make some comments around them later, but it's to give me a focus, a starting point for our next session."

"I guess that's my cue to leave, huh? Fifty minutes up?" Peter removed the cushion from behind his head, smoothed his blue jeans with it as he moved his thumbs around the floral designs. I loved watching his hands, the strong thumbs that can caress and shape uneven clay into a fine piece of art. Beautiful, smooth, dark hands that should have to do nothing but paint, sculpt, create.

"No, we still have a few minutes. How is your relationship with Lindsey these days?"

"You'll have to ask her. She's waiting in the wings."

"We have time. I'm asking you."

"Lindsey loves me, or maybe *she's* addicted too," Peter laughed. "She takes care of me. I don't deserve it."

"How is that?"

"Because I treat her like dirt sometimes, like old clay under the fingernails."

"Old clay is pretty special, isn't it?"

"Maybe. I still drink too much."

"That's contraindicated while on medication."

"I know. I know all of this. Don't go to a bar, don't drink, don't let it snowball past no return. I know not to hurt her, and I don't mean to. I just do. Then I feel guilty."

"Are you familiar with the term co-dependent?"

"Yes, I've read *the book*. Lindsey's father was an alcoholic. We've both read all of the stuff. She feeds on my weakness, and my guilt, right?"

"Does she?"

"Maybe so. Maybe if she'd just let me fall on my face in a ditch and let me stay there, we'd both be better off."

"Is that how you really feel?"

"No, I'm glad she cares enough to drag me out of a bar at 3 a.m., or out of my truck, tuck me in bed, and yell at me until I pass out, and through the next day. I'm glad she cares enough to do that." Peter laughed, stretched his legs, and stood up. "Well, Doctor Kline, I'm inclined to leave you now. I've done enough damage for one day. I'll tell Lindsey you'll be out to get her in what, ten minutes?"

"Damage? Is that how you see these sessions?"

"It was a joke. Does every word have to mean something?" he asked.

"Oh I believe they do, don't you?" I walked with Peter to the desk out front, patted his back, the crisp white shirt I'm sure Lindsey had ironed for him. He smelled like soap, clean. His light brown hair glistened. The sunlight from the office window danced in soft wisps of hair around his face, the rest of his thick mane pulled tight in a pony tail between his shoulders. I noticed a slight twitch below his left cheek bone, above the sturdy chiseled features of a man who appeared strong and in control. I left him to make another appointment and went back to my office to have a cup of coffee before asking Lindsey to come in. I knew she was waiting on the other side of the waiting room partitions, probably thumbing through a magazine or a book on co-dependency.

I sat in my office and doodled, as Peter would have it. I smiled, knowing that I had in the past scrawled a few circles, faces, curls, or zig zags to relieve my tensions from the incessant chatter of a patient I didn't particularly like or who bored me to tears. Pretending to take careful notes while "doodling" didn't happen that often. I was usually in control, remaining quite the professional, even on days I felt like crying myself.

I drew a triangle, or a pyramid, with Penelope at the topmost point and Peter and Lindsey at the bottom corners. It seemed strange for a moment that I hadn't placed Peter on top. He was, after all, the focus of attention. Then I drew another triangle, linking it to that one, like a musical instrument or another link in the chain of Peter's existence. I had intended to put him at the top with his mother and ex-wife at the bottom corners. But, again, I wrote Penelope on the uppermost point. I was confused for a moment but knew, in any case, that one triangle of women would not suffice. I had a fleeting moment of enlightenment that the particularly damaging thread of Penelope, or her essence, ran through the lot of them.

There was Peter's mother who had abandoned him when he was twelve. He never used that term or blamed her. He seemed to remember only the good years with her and blamed his father, a rigid inflexible man who refused to allow Peter's mother to be a part of her son's life ever again. She had been the one to leave, and that was that. I'm sure her flight to freedom, away from a domineering religious fanatic was a high price to pay. Peter had left his father when he turned eighteen and had never returned home or tried to find his mother.

Peter's ex-wife, June, had given him two children; both he'd said were attempts to get him to straighten up and stay home. He couldn't, even though Brandi and Daniel were the center of his life. June tortured him from time to time by not allowing him to have them on holidays, or any time after he'd failed to make child support payments.

Peter's latest lover, Lindsey, a beautiful young woman of twenty-seven, with strawberry blonde hair, bright green eyes, perfect complexion and figure, could not hold his attentions or his

B.K Smith

heart because that, according to Peter, belonged to only one woman—Penelope.

Peter had met Penelope while working on the set of a community production of the play *Tallu*. He was painting the backdrops and doing the artwork for the stage. Penelope was casting and directing. Peter swore it had been love at first . . .

My phone rang and startled me. It was Lynn, our receptionist, telling me that my four o'clock had just inquired about her appointment. I glanced at my watch—4:20. "I'm sorry," I said. "I was catching up on my notes. I'll be right out."

I left Peter's file, along with my notes, with Lynn at the desk and walked to the waiting area to find Lindsey sitting on her hands. "I'm doing great with the fingernails, Dr. Kline. I just sit on them when I have the urge to trim." Lindsey laughed as she jumped up and joined me.

I have had only four sessions with her, but each one has been a delight. She is so funny. "That's wonderful. I'm proud of you. Did Peter leave?" I asked as we moved into my office and settled in.

"He *said* he was going down the street to the bookstore, but my bet is he'll head for the bar a couple of blocks over."

"Is he drinking a lot?" I asked.

"Enough. Most days he does great on the Prozac. Everything'll be going along roses, and then he'll just disappear for hours. He might come home at three the next morning or not at all if I don't go find him."

"How do you feel about that?"

"How do you think I feel? I hate it. It makes me as mad as hell!"

"Good," I said. "What makes you feel that you have to find him?"

"Somebody does, I guess. He might hurt himself. Do you know that song about whiskey by Highway 101?"

"No, which song?"

"You know, it says something like whiskey, if you were a woman, I could fight you and get you out of his tangled mind for good? It's like I have to fight two demons—the booze and Penelope. I think it's a losing battle."

"What makes your battle?"

"Well, it's obvious that I love him, isn't it? And, besides, he doesn't have anywhere else to go. My studio is his only home."

"Tell me about the studio. What's it like?" I asked.

"Well, it's really just a warehouse, but it's huge with four big sections. There's one where I work and keep my ceramic molds and kiln, and one where Peter sculpts, paints, and creates his gargantuan art."

"What do you mean by *gargantuan?*"

"Some of the panels, like the one with Brandi and Daniel on it, are ten feet tall. He calls it 'The Lost Children.' And he works on a lot of backdrops for plays in there."

"Interesting. Describe the other rooms."

"The back section is more or less a play room. It's got a basketball goal, toys, and a stage set that Peter made for the kids. They have plays back there."

"Who has plays?"

"Peter and the kids. He makes up skits for them, and they act them out. They drove me crazy when they were here this weekend. Everything was plike this and plike that. Brandi made Daniel cry when she hit him with a magic wand. She told him she was Queen, and he was a frog prince. I think he wanted to be King, so he got a little ticked off."

"What does plike mean?" I asked.

"Oh, you know, play like. They do that all the time. It drives me nuts. Peter just goes right along with them."

"Let's see now, Brandi is eight and Daniel is five?"

"Right. They are so beautiful, but Peter spoils them rotten. I guess we both do because we don't see them that often."

"Sounds like you care deeply for them."

"They both look exactly like Peter, except Brandi has darker hair. What do you think? They're adorable."

"And this is your studio, or warehouse?"

"Well, I rent it."

"What's the fourth section like?"

"It's really divided into two parts. Out front there's a display window and tables for my ceramics, and behind that wall is where we sleep. We've got two small bedrooms, a tiny kitchen with a microwave, hot plate, and refrigerator, and an even smaller bathroom with a shower. But Peter is extending that now that we bought the old blue bathtub at a yard sale."

"Tell me about it."

"Well, it's great. It's one of those with legs. Peter hooked up everything and put it up on a platform. I bathed him in it last night."

"Bathed him?" I asked. Before, Peter had said that he loved

to wash Lindsey's hair.

"Yes. He'd been grinding and carving a magnificent madonna holding the Christ child, from an old headstone, and he was covered in white powder. It was all over him, in his eyelashes, matted in his hair, so I bathed him."

For a few moments I was lost in Lindsey's vivid descriptions of bathing Peter, this ritual they seemed to share often, washing one another's hair, smoothing, soothing each other's skin and washing away the pains of another day. I could see his blue eyes, made even darker and bluer by the fine white powder in his lashes. I imagined his head bent, the long hair hanging loosely as she tenderly massaged away the tangles there and in his mind. I could feel his strong shoulders, the warm water easing down his back beneath her loving hands.

"I use Wesson Oil," Lindsey brought me back to the office with a laugh.

"Wesson Oil?" I asked, still a little dreamy.

"We can't afford a fancy hot oil treatment every time his hair gets matted with clay or paint, so I heat up some Wesson oil in the microwave. I massage it through the mats and kinks. It works like a charm."

"Do these baths take away some of your tensions?" I asked.

"They really do. Sometimes I get so mad at him, like one night last week when he didn't come home. The next day I just shook him and shook him, and I wanted to kill him. But I kept thinking the whole time I was shaking him how pretty he was—his lips, his eyes, his face. I can't stay mad at him, especially when I'm bathing his body, touching him, so close to him just in that one moment when he's mine. I can control him."

Lindsey and I discussed the reasons for her need to control Peter, her need to feel control in all areas of her life. I gave her a few suggestions about how she might handle his next disappearing act while she twirled the long, blonde braid of hair on her right shoulder. She said she would try, but her last words to me on the way out of my office were, "I guess you think I'm wrong to put up with Peter, don't you, Dr. Kline? But if I ran him off, I'd just have to find him."

* * * *

Session # 23

"I think I just don't care anymore," Peter said as he sat across from me, pulling at the thin outer edges of the cloth pillow he always toyed with during his visits. He looked beaten and tired, dark circles spreading like bruises under his sad blue eyes. His clothing, a wrinkled grey workshirt and paint-spattered jeans, was as disheveled as his unshaved face and unwashed hair.

"You don't care about yourself?" I asked.

"About anything."

"Tell me what's happened."

"I haven't slept. I was out all night. Can you tell?" Peter managed a weak smile. Lindsey had been right. As terrible as he should've looked to me, all I could see was this pretty man.

"No. I love your fashionable combat boots. And aren't those *authentic* painters' pants?" I tried to get him to smile again.

"Sure. I didn't want to come today. Lindsey dragged me over here."

"Is there a particular reason that you didn't want to come?"

"It's all a waste I think. I've done everything you suggested. It's not working. I wrote the letter to Penelope—six pages. I told her everything I've felt for three years, the good and the bad, and how I hate the way she's treated me. Then I read it out loud and burned it, just like you said."

"Tell me a little more about it. When did you do this?"

"Last week. I wrote it. Lindsey went with me, you know, to that special place down by the river, the hill, with all the trees."

"Yes I remember," I said. Peter had described this secret place several times, so vividly that I felt I had been there. A soft grassy hill buried deep within birches, pines, and oaks, a private view of the river that no one ever saw, according to Peter, except for him and his secret love Penelope during their infrequent rendezvous by boat. It could not be seen from the river—was hidden, obstructed, and guarded as deeply as his passion.

Peter went on, "I read the letter to Lindsey and we played a song called 'Can You Take Me High Enough' while the letter burned. I even let some balloons go. Lindsey's idea. We wrote the name Penelope on five blue ones and Peter on a red one. When we let them fly, to go in different directions, the one with my name on it popped. Can you believe it? We just sat there looking at it on the ground—like pieces of an exploded toy heart. And we looked up and down, at the ones going up over the trees until they looked like little dots in the clouds, then back down to the slivers of red rubber on the ground. It was like watching a tennis match. We felt like fools, but we got tickled at ourselves."

B.K Smith

"Did you feel some sense of freedom or release from Penelope?" I asked.

"Sure, for that day I did. I felt great, free from her. There was this beautiful full moon later, and I made love to Lindsey."

"Well, I'd say that's a step forward—in yours and Penelope's special place?"

"I was being defiant, I guess. I didn't even let it make me feel guilty too much."

"Too much?" I asked.

"Some." Peter grinned.

"And you never made love to Penelope there did you?" I knew he hadn't, that Penelope had never allowed him the pleasure. I knew she had promised him, teased him, allowed him to go just so far in that naturalness by the river, in the middle of all that life and energy, before she used her husband as an excuse to deaden his desire.

"You know that we didn't." Peter sounded offended.

"Do you think that was natural?"

"Of course I don't. But what choice did I have? She said she couldn't until after the divorce. Dr. Kline, I have made love to Penelope in every way two people or souls could possibly imagine. I have touched her, danced with her, held her close to me, and kissed those soft lips, the softest I'll ever know. And I've carried on long conversations, maybe years or centuries, with those deep brown eyes, so dark sometimes that they seem to turn black and swallow me up."

"Describe Penelope's physique."

"Perfect. About five-three, slim. Why? You know that."

"Did you ever feel the urge to coerce her into giving in to you?"

"I pushed too far sometimes. She seems small and fragile, but she's strong and stubborn, and that voice, those soft sweet words, always promised that it would be soon." Peter was shaking a little, and a deep red flush began at the base of his neck and spread to his face. It amazed me that this woman who was two hours away, this woman he hadn't even seen in almost a year, could evoke such reaction from his autonomic nervous system and could control his emotions from such a distance. Peter was trembling, and tears made his eyes a brighter blue. I took off my jacket, walked over to him, and covered his chest and arms.

"Are you cold?"

"I don't know."

"I'm so glad you're getting in touch with your feelings just at this moment," I said, as I patted his shoulder before returning to my chair across from him.

"There are two voices, you know," Peter said as he flicked a tear away from his cheek. I wanted him to let them go. I wanted to comfort him and tell him it was okay to let it all go. I knew in that moment I would find a way to free him from his past hurts and disappointments. It seemed a certainty.

"Explain the voices," I said.

"One is like a siren. It's sweet and tempting. It's like I'm shipwrecked and she sings to me from way out there in the ocean. I get caught up in the music and the myth. She dances close to me, makes love to me with her words. I can't get back. I need a lighthouse to bring me home. Are you my lighthouse, Dr. Kline?"

"That's a flattering image. I'd love to think so. But you can get back all by yourself once you realize she's a flesh and blood woman with real problems and real fears of her own. And, Peter, I don't believe after all this time that she's going to leave her husband, do you?"

"No, I guess I don't. She kept telling me that when Jeremy graduated, she'd be free; she'd feel okay about leaving."

"Jeremy is her son, isn't he? He's eighteen now?"

"Yes. I saw her for the last time last summer, on June 23, remember? When she told me that she and her *partner* were going to try and make it a little longer."

"Yes, I remember. But she still contacts you, doesn't she?"

"Even more so when she thinks I'm pulling away for good. It's like she has radar or something. She knows when I'm really trying to break away and let go. The day after I burned the letter, she called."

"You didn't tell me that."

"I didn't tell you because you advised no contact, abstain, remember? I should've hung up on her. She'll be forty next month. I can't even tell her happy birthday."

"Does that explain your dark mood? Because she called again?"

"I guess. There was that sweet voice on the phone. She acted like nothing has changed. I know she wants me to go back to being her wind-up toy. She won't carry on a real conversation. She just wants me to keep playing in this fantasy world when and if she chooses the time and place. It drives me crazy."

"You mentioned there were two voices. Describe the other one."

B.K Smith

"The other one? It's the voice of a coward, and it's silent—deadly silent," Peter whispered the last two words.

"You mean because she doesn't call or write to you for months at a time?"

"Yes, and when I do hear from her, she won't answer my questions. The game playing is loud and clear. It's reality that's as dead as a broken balloon. I feel dead today. I've lost three years of my life—some months I don't even remember. I've just waited in some dark heavy place."

"How dark is that place right now?"

"The darkest."

"Describe it for me."

"Very dark. Dangerous. I can't breathe. I don't even care if I breathe. It takes too much effort. I know I'm falling deeper. I can feel each level drop with a thud like somebody's dumping heavy loads of clay on me every few minutes, going down, dark."

I didn't like the way Peter was talking. It disturbed me. I hadn't realized just how far his depression had advanced. He was so hard to read during some sessions. "Peter, do you think you might hurt yourself?"

"I wouldn't feel a thing. How could it hurt? Bang, it's over."

"Would you spend a few days in the hospital? I can see you every day. It's only a mile from here."

"No. I can't do that."

"Why not?"

"I've got art classes starting at the college next week. I need the money."

"This is important. I'm talking about your life."

"Well, if I'm going to live I need money, right? Lindsey and I are broke. Today will be her last session with you. She wants me to keep coming. That's all we can afford. I certainly can't afford a hospital. I'll live."

"Will you?"

"I will. I will. I promise." Peter rolled his eyes and crossed his heart.

"Okay, if no hospital, I'll give you another option."

"Oh really?"

"Yes, I'm very serious. I want you to make sure that you are with someone, Lindsey, for the next 72 hours. Don't be alone. Will you promise me that?"

"Promise."

"And you'll call me if you need me, at any hour? I don't usually give my home number to clients, but I will give it to you now and expect you to call if you're in trouble, okay?"

"Yes yes yes," Peter said as I wrote my number on a slip of paper and gave it to him.

"And I want you to do something else, another option," I said.

"What?"

"I want you to call Penelope and ask her to come to your next session. I think it's time we made her part of the solution. I believe there has to be a face-to-face resolution here before you can go on. Do you think she will help you?"

"I have no idea. I'll try. I can't follow this, first abstain, then see her."

"I know the psychic energy that will be generated from the anticipation of seeing her will keep you alive. That's what I'm interested in now."

"Is that a fact?"

"You'd better believe it. So do we have a deal? You'll do what I've asked?"

"Like I said, I'll try but I doubt that she'll come," Peter said as he stood up and moved toward the door ahead of me. "Oh, by the way, Doc, I have a what did you call it before—a 'doorknob disclosure' for you: I'm having a heart attack. Shouldn't we talk about it?"

I slapped Peter's shoulder. He laughed and tried to seem in control with his attempt at humor before he left. I had told him once about how patients sometimes extended their sessions with a last-minute disclosure that couldn't wait. He tried to joke, but I knew he probably wanted to stay in the safety of my office a little longer. I hated to see him go that day. I wanted to protect him from the hurts to come.

I sat in my office before asking Lindsey to come in, and I wondered if I'd made the right decision. If Penelope did come with Peter to his next session, I wasn't sure what would happen. I was confident that the meeting would take care of itself. Penelope might answer Peter's questions, and if she didn't, he would be able to confront her on neutral ground and, hopefully, see her in a real situation for the first time. Maybe he would finally realize her flaws.

I had mixed feelings about what I'd done, but my guess was that Penelope would not show at all. The cut would be deep and cruel for Peter, to know that his Penelope would be such a coward that she would not help him at all, that, in fact, she had never loved him. For Peter, this would sever all hopes of having her and all ties to her. He could finally let her go, and we could explore the there and then of his past rather than the here and now. Only at that point could Peter really begin to heal because I was convinced his depression and obsessions had begun somewhere back in time, with his parents, in a dysfunctional and destructive family relationship. Peter would heal. He would realize his own inner strength.

* * * *

When Lindsey made herself comfortable in my office, I said, "You mentioned last session that you might not be able to continue therapy. What are your plans?"

"I can't keep coming. We're broke. Or I'm broke. I have to take care of us pretty much. A lot of Peter's money goes for child support. But he needs to keep seeing you. He's way down right now. Don't you think?" Lindsey looked pretty haggard herself. Her soft young complexion never needed makeup, but she looked pale, and her green eyes didn't shine as they usually did.

"Right now I think I want to talk about you. How are you feeling about paying the way?"

"I wish he'd help me more. Hell, I owe my right leg to Sears. I've bought him all kinds of tools—air compressors, routers, and Mikita saws so he can work. All of my credit cards are maxed out."

"What does Peter say about all these gifts?"

"He thanks me, of course, but he never *asks* me for anything, so I can't really get mad at him can I? Like this morning I jumped on him when he finally came in. I was ready to tear into him for staying out all night. I sat on his stomach and beat him over the head with a French book I'd bought him."

"A French book?" I asked.

"Yes. A few months ago he'd said he wanted to learn French. So, I took it upon myself to buy him a book. This morning I screamed at him that he'd never once even picked it up. I hit him with it over and over."

"How did Peter react?"

"He just held his arm over his face, that beautiful face that I love even when I'm pounding at it with any available object."

"Does Peter ever offer any explanations, or any help?" I asked.

"Peter tells me I'd be better off without him and that he should leave."

"And you don't want to let him go?"

"No. I can't. He has no place to go. He wouldn't even eat if

I didn't make sure that he did. And I love him, Dr. Kline. He can be so sweet and giving when I'm not yelling at him. We always end up in bed no matter how bad the fight was."

"Can you see a dependent relationship in which you function as a rescuer?"

"Sure I can. I feed him, bathe him, bring him coffee to the blue throne bathtub, serve him, console him, and bring him home from bars."

"How do you feel about serving him?"

"Most days I love taking care of him. I feel like I'm supporting a starving artist," Lindsey laughed and went on. "I go all over the place looking for things to help him sculpt or paint. Last week I drove all over town gathering up old marble headstones."

"Headstones, as from cemeteries?"

"Yes. Some places sell them real cheap. He can take an old piece of stone and carve out a gorgeous Adam and Eve or these fish sculptures that look ancient and valuable. He's amazing."

"Lindsey, what are you getting from all of this?"

"I feel as if I'm contributing to art. Peter is a true artist. He is art."

Lindsey's observation seemed on target. Peter was beautiful, not just his face, his eyes, or his smooth sure hands, but his soul as well. There was an indefinable grace in the midst of his suffering. It was so hard for me at times to deal with his problems on a clinical level. He was beyond textbook categorizations or treatments. I think I had been afraid at times to upset his artistic center, that delicate balance of art and reality. His essence seemed so fragile and ethereal.

"I'm afraid he'll leave me, Dr. Kline."

"Leave you?" I had to get back to Lindsey.

"Yes. I've done all this for him, and I'm afraid that if he does become a success later on, he'll leave me."

"Are you willing to take that chance?"

"I don't have any choice. I'd be miserable without him."

"Are you happy, Lindsey? Do you know what it would take to make you really happy?"

"Not much. I mean, just average stuff, enough money to pay the rent, be comfortable, buy art supplies, good coffee, and to know Peter could love me like he's loved Penelope."

"You have never said much about Penelope."

"I try not to think about her. He met her right before his divorce, or should I say was mesmerized by her, caught in her web.

I've never understood the attraction or the charm. I mean, she's eleven years older than Peter. I think he was looking for a mother. Penelope is just another unfinished piece of work."

"What do you mean?"

"He has a hard time finishing things—his marriage—and most of his work. I'm the one to push him to finish a sculpture or a painting usually. He wants perfection, and I don't think he believes he can ever create anything good enough."

"You knew Peter loved Penelope when you met him two years ago. What motivates you to stay with him?" I asked.

"Because I knew she was beyond his reach too. I knew she'd never leave her husband. I certainly wanted to help him finish that one. I thought he'd change."

"And speaking of change, Lindsey, our time is almost up, and I'd like to change your mind if I can about seeing me again. I'm sure we can work something out financially, and I'd like to shift directions if we can. I want to talk about you, your life, *your* family, and know you separate from Peter."

"I'll never be separate from Peter, Dr. Kline. He is my life. He is me. It takes the two of us to finish a work, or to create something good and whole."

"Sounds as though you love Peter very much," I said, feeling Lindsey's complete devotion to her young man, the artist.

"Yes I do. He's special, Dr. Kline. A couple of days ago I watched him work from the doorway into his section of the studio. He had opened the big doors on the side of the warehouse so he could get the late afternoon light and breezes. I watched him smooth the clay hard with his thumbs one moment and then ease his forefinger around the strong legs of one of the running men on the bas-relief. I thought those Greek gods didn't hold a candle to him. He was so handsome and strong, and the light around him made him look surreal, almost Christ-like, sacrificing, giving himself up to his work. Excuse me if I'm being too melodramatic." Lindsey seemed a little embarrassed and thought she needed to relieve the moment with a laugh.

Then she went on, "The mood was broken, of course, when the mean snippy little voice came over the intercom at the Dairy Queen behind the warehouse, 'Kin I hep you?' I got tickled and Peter realized I was behind him. He grinned and said, 'Kin I hep you, Miss?' Dr. Kline, Peter and I aren't perfect, but I believe we can be happy together. If I love him this much, how can it not work eventually?"

"I believe you can do anything, Lindsey. I think you can make anything work," I said as I walked with her out of my office. We said goodbye, and she said she'd think about coming back. I hoped that she would. I knew I would miss her, this loving young woman whose generosity and unselfishness could heal the world if her gifts were packaged for humanity. I realized that she could certainly help Peter to heal and that, in fact, it was she who was his lighthouse, guiding his way back.

* * * *

Session #24

I checked the waiting room at half past noon, hoping Penelope would be early for the one o'clock appointment. Peter had called a week before to reschedule and said that Penelope would be meeting him at my office. He said she needed to come on a particular day when she wasn't teaching during her spring break. His voice had been hopeful, excited, when he told me, "She said she thinks the meeting is a good idea, Doc. Can you believe it? She's coming."

I scanned the waiting room fifteen minutes later. Peter knew we wouldn't begin until after one. I wanted a few minutes alone with Penelope. I would know her in an instant—the dark brooding eyes, the sensuous mouth, the thick black hair touched with elegant brush strokes of gray, and cut short, soft around her ears. I looked for the small, strong body that had made Peter ache and dream. I wanted to invite her into my office, hear the haunting voice of Peter's illusion, and decide how to filter it for him in the session to come.

I would ask her how she enjoyed teaching French, and why she chose the language. I would ask her about her family, her son, all the while sculpting my own image of this woman's reality. She would probably be a little nervous, knowing she had begun a fantasy that was out of control, that she could no longer hurt Peter. Why else would she come. He would enter the office, and she would offer him one last enchanting smile. I would not let it melt his heart again.

I checked the waiting area a last time at one o'clock. No one. I walked to my office to observe the busy highway just beyond the dogwoods. Then I walked to a window in the reception area that overlooks the parking lot. I saw Peter sitting in his truck. Several minutes passed before he got out. He leaned against the door, his eyes searching the lot. I knew Penelope wasn't coming. I had to

B.K Smith

gather my wits, focus on Peter, and determine how to ease him through this final disappointment. It would be the last day of their acquaintance, and resolution would come in the days to follow. The cut would be deep and precise.

Peter reached into the truck for his sketchbook and journal, the two items I had asked him to bring to several sessions, and then he walked into the building. I met him in the waiting area.

"Is she here?" he asked.

"I haven't seen her."

"She's probably stuck in traffic," Peter said as he walked with me to my office. "There was a jam at the Nashville exit."

"Well maybe she'll be here in a few minutes," I said. "I've told the girls at the desk to look for her and bring her to my office. We'll talk until she gets here, okay?"

Peter sat down but not for long. "That's her car," he said, as he shot up to the window. "I'm sure that's it. I hope she knows where to turn. The street signs are crossed out front; did you know that? The one at the end of those trees, just as you turn in. I'll go check the parking lot."

Peter returned in a few minutes. I checked my watch—half past one. He slumped on the couch. "It wasn't her, I guess, unless she missed the turn. This place is hard to find."

"I know," I said, "and I'll check with someone about those street signs. What have you got there?"

"I sketched something for Penelope. Some kind of self portrait from hell, I guess. I don't know what I'd call it. Here, Lindsey wrote a poem to go with it." Peter handed me a sheet of paper from his journal.

"Why don't you read it to me?" I asked.

"Not right now. You keep it if you want." I slid the poem inside my notebook. Peter's face was flushed, and his right hand gripped the pillow next to him, his knuckles white.

"Have you written in your journal?"

"Not much. Where is she? Is she lost? What time is it?" He slammed the sketch pad and journal under the couch.

"It's one thirty-five," I answered.

"Tell me what Penelope said when you called her." I knew Peter was extremely agitated. I wanted to calm him.

"Oh, she was in this great mood. She was laughing about my fishing boat and comparing it to a gondola. She said she couldn't wait to float along *our* canals to *our* Venice."

"Your place on the river?"

"Yes. See, she was acting like nothing has changed, like she hasn't ignored my existence for months. She can't see where I've been."

"You mean in that dark heavy place?"

"Dark and deadly."

"What did she say about the appointment for today?"

"I told you, don't you listen? Doesn't anything I say ever mean anything to anybody? She was happy about the idea. She thought it was great, great, great!"

"Of course what you say matters. I remember. I just thought she might have told you something you forgot to mention— something that could be important to us."

"Important?" Peter clinched his fists and his teeth as he began to grind out the words. "Nothing is. I'm not. Only Penelope matters to Penelope. She's not coming for me. She won't be here or anywhere ever. She never has been there or here for me. She never will be."

"It's two o'clock, Peter. Is there some way you could check to see why she didn't come?" I asked.

"I can't call her at home, and she's not at work. I'll call Lindsey and see if she left a message."

"Would she do that with Lindsey there?"

"She's called before when *she* wanted to. She doesn't care about Lindsey's feelings either. Could I use your phone?"

"Of course."

Peter called the studio and asked Lindsey if there had been any messages. I assumed there had been when he said, "Is that all? What else did she say? Okay, no, I'm okay. I'll be home in a little while. We're done here." Peter was not shaking, not flushed, and he didn't seem angry at all when he hung up the phone and collapsed on the couch. His face appeared drained, his blue eyes dull and vacant, void of any reaction or feeling at all.

"What?" I asked.

"There was a message on the answering machine when Lindsey got back from lunch with her sister."

"What was it?"

"Penelope said, 'I've had a change of heart. I won't be at the meeting today. There's no need to return this call.' That's all, Doc, all she said. No explanations. Nothing. And she left it after she knew I'd be gone. Change of heart? I don't think she has one."

"How will you handle this, Peter? Tell me what you'll do when you leave here."

"What do you mean?"

"Will you drink?"

"No, I won't do that."

"Good," I said. "Will you drive fast?"

"Probably."

"That's not okay."

"Okay, I won't. I'll just go home I guess." He stood up and headed toward the door, his steps heavy and slow.

"You're going to be fine, Peter. I want you to call me tomorrow, okay? I want to see you again in a few days. Will you do that?"

"Sure."

"You're okay. You're stronger than you think. You'll be okay."

"I'm going home," Peter said, with just a whisper of resolution in his voice. I knew that sound would become more audible in the days to come, would resonate, become loud and clear to his own ears and spirit.

"Yes, go home. It's a good place to be right now, isn't it? Lindsey's there, waiting in the wings. In fact, I think she just may be wearing them, don't you?"

With a faint smile, almost unnoticeable, and an ever so small glint of hope in his tired blue eyes, Peter left my office. I knew I would worry, but not so much. Penelope would soon become a past he could forget. He would welcome the forgetting. She would become no more important than a stranger passing by him on the street. This would happen in a very short time. And I knew that it was time, also, to urge him back into another past, time that he found his mother and time to resolve those confusions. We would move slowly toward that resolution in days to come.

I had no more appointments because I had saved a big block of time for Penelope and Peter in case it had been necessary. I got a cup of coffee and sat down to make my notes when I realized Peter had left his journal and sketch book. I thumbed through his journal. The last few pages were filled with scattered and fragmented thoughts, poetry.

I am dead when
she refuses to strike
blows to my head,
cocking the gun

to render me
frozen.

She loves me Russian roulette.

I click the chambers.
Which one will fire
her oblivious.

The words bothered me, not because I thought they might sound suicidal. I was sure Peter was beyond that point, if he'd ever really been there at all. I was concerned, as always, if I had made the right decisions. So many artistic people visit that dark, heavy place, sometimes, I'm convinced, to dance in the shadows of creativity. Penelope had been Peter's angst, his siren, and his dark muse. Was I right to push him to sever that mysterious, mystical bond? I hoped so. I felt more confident when I observed the sketch Peter had done for Penelope, and when I read the poem Lindsey had written to accompany it. Her words had captured the essence of the work perfectly.

The Last Poem from Hell

Possession is nine tenths of my life.
She has claimed this lost
dark soul.
And I imagine her laughter
resting just above my cage.
She'll kick it now and then,
or toss me a small piece
of delicious meat.
Then she's gone.
I have progressed.
No longer do I suffer from depression
or obsession.
Those are simple maladies.
I bang my head bloody
against the bars, hard
skin softened by days
of uselessness.
I vomit, casting my nets into
the abyss.

B.K Smith

Outside there is blue sky,
the purest blue,
and lush green trees
and blue eyes looking
back at me.

I was sure Lindsey had been right. It really would take both of them to create a whole, to complete a work as complex and as beautiful as life. And they would have a life together, one sculpted from lots of love, and tempered by the elusive shadows of art—unattainable, yet complete.

THE POETESS

My Atlantis. She takes me down below the ocean, past the blue-winged fishes. Deeper and deeper through undercaves, my body sinks and glides against the shelf moss. I watch the air bubbles burst on pink tentacles of ancient plants and mammals buried far beneath the uneasy roll of waves. And I rest on the bottom, away from the sounds, blind as the inhabitants, and buried in the dark, cool depths of the lyrics. My body is weightless, curling up like thin patterns of smoke, drifting down again to merge level with the velvet floor.

"The Masos are angry today. Someone took their tickets. You should stay off the streets," says the poetess. And she stamps approval on my papers.

"But what about the score? The assembly says it's no good."

"I have seen worse," she says.

"I don't feel like I fit in," I say.

"You don't." The poetess smiles. Her eyes grow dark, changing from brown to blue, to black. They're intense, inquisitive, knowing. They dance. There's a rhythm in her eyes and in her soft, young mouth.

"May I borrow your book?" I ask.

"Will you read it?"

In the evening I sit under the single white bulb in my room and send cigarette smoke toward the light in half circles. I stare at the walls, count the cracks in the plaster. I think of the walls crumbling around my chair in a powdered heap. I look at the cover of the book, and know I can't read it tonight. I have to improve the score. The words would interfere, envelope me, take my mind off the formulas.

I find excuses to visit the poetess, to hear her voice—the melody in her words like tempting sirens to the shipwrecked. I walk the long corridors to her room.

"Are you busy?" I ask.

"No, of course not."

"Here's your book."

"And yours when you want it."

"I was arrested today."

"Why?" she asks.

"I was sitting in a place for the maimed."

"Are you maimed?" the poetess asks.

"I don't feel well."

B.K Smith

"Take this blue stamp. They won't bother you again."

"The Masos are crying today."

"Were many killed?" she asks.

"Only a few. They jumped from their windows. They lost the game. I guess it's sad."

The poetess reads to me. I follow her to the field in natural tones. Thin, fresh grass moves around my feet. Undergrowth rises taller, pulling me by cadences. The landscape swells into forests, and I am lost in the movement of deep green shades. I feel the wet soil beneath my feet and walk slowly. The ground tugs gently at my legs, sucks my body easily into darkness. Earth smells fill my nostrils. I break into pieces—particles of land—and my body stirs with the pulse and rhythms of the underworld.

I leave relaxed, drained, exhausted. I walk the long corridors away from the poetess and into the sunlight. It hurts my eyes, feels hot on my skin. I go through the motions and try to avoid the outsiders. I don't have to fit in. I'll see her again tomorrow.

"Can I talk to you?"

"Come in," says the poetess.

"The Masos are happy today. The assembly lowered the interest to forty-six percent."

"Interesting," she says.

"I've been to the mail drop again. It was the same, the feeling of dread before I opened it. I closed my eyes and reached in. There were several this time."

"Were you afraid?" she asks.

"Not so much. They took a week's pay, and cancelled the extra job. They refused my last request."

"The yellow ones are the worst, aren't they?" she asks.

"I need your help. I haven't any money, nor food in the house," I say.

"Take this. It should help."

I can't believe her generosity. She gives me more than enough. I touch her hand. It feels like silk, but strong, and I want to hold on. A small, blue vein crosses the back, from knuckle to wrist. Her blood flows there beneath the softness. I want to join the red rich stream.

The poetess recites words she hasn't written. The air around me whistles, making the mellow sounds of a flute. I fall into a vacuum, a space. Underneath is night, and the faint reflections of stars miles below. I like the quiet—soundless except for a distant twinkle against the air, and my breathing.

The poetess is silent. She says the new words will take time. I leave her again, but promise to return. My room is lonely. My bed is dry and hot. An insect drags its brittle legs across my own in the dark. I'm afraid, and I reach for the words to hold against me. My hand touches nothing but the lukewarm glass of water I brought to bed. I lift it to my parched lips for a drink. The water smells. Like water after the goldfish have died.

I have no excuses for her this time. I walk along the streets and decide what to say. The Masos are restless. Caleb is coming. They've written it everywhere. They're not saying much, only skulking in the doorways and talking in whispers. I could tell her that.

The corridors are different. They seem shorter. The rooms look unfamiliar, and there's an uneasiness in the hallways. I walk to her door. A new name runs along the bottom of the glass. *Dr. Rochambeau.* I knock.

"Enter."

"Where is she?" I ask.

"She's gone."

"But she's teaching me."

"Are you here about the score? It's no good. It doesn't meet our requirements. I'm afraid we'll have to let you go." The man doesn't look up. He presses a pen hard against a yellow pad and tosses a cigar around in his mouth with tongue and teeth.

"Can you read?" I ask.

"Of course, I can read."

"Can you recite?"

"Recite what? 'Four score and seven years ago.' That what you want? Here take this book. It has your name on it. Run along now. I have work to do."

I walk the corridors, but not to the end where the sun begins much sooner now. I slip down into a dark, empty corner and open the book. *My Atlantis. She takes me down below the ocean, past the blue-winged fishes. Deeper and deeper into undercaves my body sinks.*

Biography

B.K. *(Karen) Smith received her Master of Fine Arts degree in creative writing from the University of Alabama in 1983. Since then she has been teaching at Bevill State Community College—and writing in Jasper, Alabama, where she lives with her Persian cat Brandy and several fictional characters.*

Her short stories have appeared twice in The Sucarnochee Review, *and both her fiction and poetry have appeared in* Voices & Visions.

Her future plans include moving into a lighthouse, writing, and living happily on into the hereafter.